The Great Expanding Guinea Pig
&
Beware of the Snowblobs!

You, me and Thing

KAREN
McCOMBIE

ff

FABER & FABER

First published in 2014
by Faber and Faber Limited
Bloomsbury House,
74–77 Great Russell Street,
London, WC1B 3DA

Typeset by Faber and Faber
Printed in England by CPI Group (UK) Ltd, Croydon, CR0 4YY

A CIP record for this book
is available from the British Library

ISBN 978–0–571–31055–5

FSC
www.fsc.org
MIX
Paper from
responsible sources
FSC® C101712

2 4 6 8 10 9 7 5 3 1

For Dylan, Erin and Jess, who like Thing very, very much (it likes you, too!)

Have you read all of Ruby, Jackson and Thing's adventures?

Contents

The Great Expanding Guinea Pig

You, me and Thing

Contents

A super-mega, EXTRAORDINARY Thing

Boo!!

There – got your attention.

It's just that I have an exciting story you might like to hear.

So, where should I start?

By introducing myself, I guess.

I am Ruby Morgan.

I am ten years old.

I am an ordinary girl, who lives in an ordinary house, with an ordinary family (one mum, one dad, one extremely old cat).

'Yeah, well, *that* doesn't sound too exciting so far,' I hear you all cry.

Ah, but my story gets better.

Lots better.

AND weirder.

Honest.

Mainly because of my super-mega, *extraordinary* secret . . .

But, hey, let's begin at the beginning.

Once upon a not-very-long-ago time, the cottage where I live sat on the edge of a huge wood.

Then someone decided it might be nicer to get rid of all those pesky trees, and build a huge housing estate there instead.

(BAD idea, if you ask me.)

All that's left of lovely Muir Woods are five straggly trees bunched at the end of my garden.

Oh, and the super-mega, extraordinary secret.

'Yes, but what *is* it?' you might be saying, right about now.

OK, since you asked, it's a small creature called Thing, which used to live deep, deep, *deep* in the heart of Muir Woods — until the forest got eaten by chainsaws. And that's when I found Thing lost and lonely by those five straggly trees at the bottom of my garden.

'Um . . . what sort of thing *is* this Thing?' you might be wondering.

Here, let me help.

Think of a squirrel.

A red one.

Now mush it up in your mind with a tiny, talking troll.

Add weeny stubby wings that don't work, and eyes as big as moons.

Got it? A picture in your head of what Thing looks like, I mean?

Or maybe I've just given you a headache, trying to imagine all that strangeness. (And I haven't even *mentioned* the rubbish magic it can do.)

To be honest, sometimes Thing gives *me* a headache.

It's incredibly cute but also incredibly good at landing me and my friend Jackson in trouble.

Like the time we went to the Happy Valley Petting Zoo.

We got in *so* much trouble that my head nearly exploded.

A bit like the guinea pig, I suppose . . .

But, hey, I'm rushing ahead.

Let's just go back to the day when the whole great expanding guinea-pig thing started.

And it started with a cooing, pooing pigeon.

Cos if the pigeon hadn't cooed and pooed when it did, Jackson might not have spotted the dog.

And if Jackson hadn't spotted the dog, we wouldn't have gone to the Gala Day at the Happy Valley Petting Zoo.

And if we hadn't gone to the Gala Day at the Happy Valley Petting Zoo, we wouldn't have had all the fuss with the guinea pig that grew and grew and grew until . . .

Oops, I'm rushing again, aren't I?

I think I should take a big breath, and start again, this time calmly and clearly.

Up a tree . . .

2

A huff and a woof

'Ooooh, it *nice* to sit where birdies singinging!' Thing sighed happily one day, staring up into the leafiness above our heads.

And that was the day it seemed like a fun idea to climb one of the straggly trees at the bottom of my garden.

Thing scrambled up first.

Then Jackson bounded up.

Then it was *my* turn, and I found out that

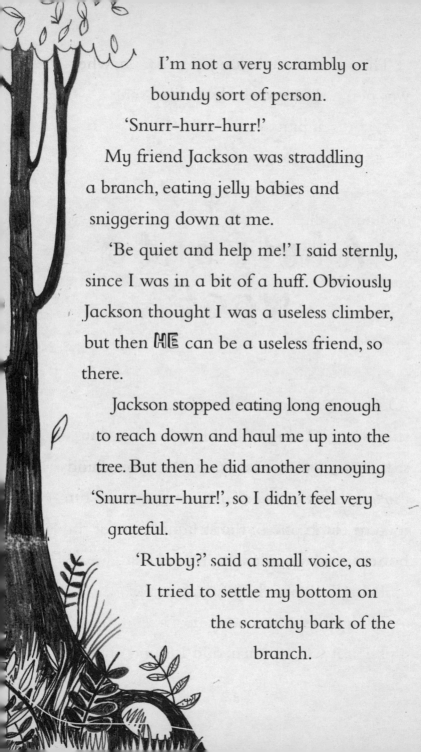

I'm not a very scrambly or
boundy sort of person.

'Snurr-hurr-hurr!'

My friend Jackson was straddling
a branch, eating jelly babies and
sniggering down at me.

'Be quiet and help me!' I said sternly,
since I was in a bit of a huff. Obviously
Jackson thought I was a useless climber,
but then HE can be a useless friend, so
there.

Jackson stopped eating long enough
to reach down and haul me up into the
tree. But then he did another annoying
'Snurr-hurr-hurr!', so I didn't feel very
grateful.

'Rubby?' said a small voice, as
I tried to settle my bottom on
the scratchy bark of the
branch.

The small voice belonged to Thing, who was perched next to Jackson like some freaky, fuzzy pigeon.

'It's *Ruby*,' I reminded Thing.

'Oh, I for*gotted*!' Thing purred apologetically.

'That's OK. Did you want to ask me something?' I said more gently, now that me and my bottom had got our balance and I didn't feel quite so huffy.

'Yes, *please*, Rubby!'

'Snurr-hurr-hurr!' sniggered Jackson.

I'd have reached over and punched him in the arm, if I wasn't worried about knocking the big donut out of the tree. (That's me – a *non*-useless, kind and caring friend.)

'So, what's your question?' I asked Thing, ignoring Jackson and his sniggering.

'Why Boy keep making *Snurr-hurr-hurr* noise?'

'Because he has a *very* small brain,' I explained.

Thing turned its huge eyes on Jackson.

Then all of a sudden it scampered straight up his arm and tried to peer in his ear.

'Gerroff!' yelped Jackson, getting prickled by Thing's claws and tickled by its fur.

'Rubby, it too *dark* to see into Boy's head – EEK!!!' Thing squeaked.

Perhaps Jackson didn't like being prickled

and tickled. Or maybe he didn't like getting his head examined. Whichever it was, he yanked poor Thing away.

'Jackson! Leave Thing alone!' I hissed.

Getting Thing stressed out is Not A Good Idea.

When Thing gets stressed, magic tends to ping and sproing from nowhere, and that *never* ends well.

'Ouch! Stop digging your claws in,' Jackson roared, as Thing now wriggled and wiggled in his hands, making him drop his packet of jelly babies.

'Not *squidging* me, Boy!' Thing squealed back.

'Shush, you two!' I muttered, feeling panicky.

It wasn't just stray, rubbish magic I was worried about. If Jackson carried on roaring and Thing carried on squeaking, it would

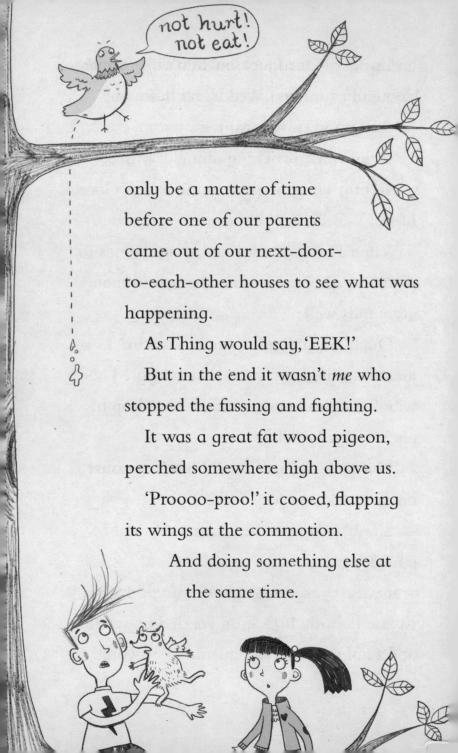

only be a matter of time before one of our parents came out of our next-door-to-each-other houses to see what was happening.

As Thing would say, 'EEK!'

But in the end it wasn't *me* who stopped the fussing and fighting.

It was a great fat wood pigeon, perched somewhere high above us.

'Proooo-proo!' it cooed, flapping its wings at the commotion.

And doing something else at the same time.

'Urgh!' groaned Jackson, as a slimy white blob landed on his gelled blond hair.

He relaxed his grip on Thing long enough for our gingery friend to scuttle over to the safety of my lap.

'Just your luck!' I laughed, as Jackson winced.

'Not *luck,* Rubby!' purred Thing. 'Pigeon thinking Boy *bad*, Pigeon shout, "Not hurt! Not eat!"'

'That bird thought I was going to *eat* you?' said Jackson, leaping down from the branch.

'Jackson would never eat you,' I reassured Thing, stroking it as it waddled anxiously from foot to tiny foot.

'Yeah! All your fur would get stuck between my teeth. Yuck!' joked Jackson, wiping his hair with a grotty-looking tissue he'd pulled out of his pocket.

'Woof!'

Jackson stopped wiping.

I stopped stroking.

Thing stopped waddling.

We had a guest in our straggle of trees . . .

'Hello there!' said Jackson, bending down and patting something I couldn't quite see.

Leaning over just enough to get a better view (but not enough to fall out of the tree), I caught sight of a black and white spaniel with its head in the packet of jelly babies.

It was wagging its tail so hard its whole back end was swaying.

'Not *like* barkers, Rubby,' whis-purred Thing, clawing its way up my chest and trembling.

'You mean dogs?' I checked.

'They too . . . *chasey*,' muttered Thing.

'Chasey?'

'They go chase, chase, chase, *bark*,' Thing explained with a shudder. 'Or chase, chase, chase, *bite*. Peh!'

'Don't worry – it's really friendly!' Jackson called to us, then burst out laughing as the dog suddenly jumped up and knocked him over with oodles of enthusiasm and licking.

'Huh-ooo!' the dog yodelled between licks.

Which gave me an idea.

Thing was so good at listening that he had learned the languages of every creature that had ever wandered through Muir Woods.

And while Thing might not be too keen on the dog, *I* was pretty keen to know what it was saying.

'What does "huh-ooo" mean?' I asked Thing.

Thing clung on to my top and peered anxiously down at Jackson and the black and white slobbery blur.

'Lost,' Thing translated.

Being flat on his back, Jackson was in the perfect position to stare up at me and Thing.

'It's lost? Hey, buddy, *are* you lost?'

'Huh-ooo!'

Jackson was also in the perfect position to check out the dangling tag on the dog's collar.

'It's name is Frodo and here's the address . . . 39 Walnut Grove.'

'That's just a few streets away on the estate,' I said. 'Let's take it ba—'

'No! *Not* leaves me, Rubby!' Thing begged, as I began to move.

'Ruby, you stay and look after Thing, and I'll take Frodo home,' said Jackson, taking off his belt, threading it through the dog's collar and turning it into a lookalike lead. 'I'll only be a few minutes.'

And off ran Jackson and Frodo, through the zigzag of streets all named after the trees that used to live here.

'I not have to see barker *again*, Rubby? It gone away now?' Thing blinked up at me with its full-moon eyes.

'Don't worry. I'm sure Frodo won't be back,' I answered my shivery little friend.

But two things *were* for sure . . .

1. We certainly hadn't seen the last of slobbery Frodo.

2. I had absolutely no idea how to get out of this stupid tree.

Well, hello again!

It had been two days since Jackson had reunited Frodo with his grateful owner.

And two days since I'd learned that 'Huh-ooo!' is dog-speak for 'lost'.

That last fact was woozling round my head when I got home from school and found my very ancient cat Christine awake and hunched upright on my bed.

Normally, Christine cat spends her time

happily sleeping, snoozing or dozing in comfy circles. Awake and hunched upright was **ALL** wrong.

'Maybe she's coming down with something,' Mum suggested, when I called her upstairs. 'Or maybe she's just getting old and poorly, Ruby. If she's still the same tomorrow, we can take her to the vet . . .'

After Mum went downstairs, I sat on the bed, stroking Christine and wondering what was up.

I thought about gently poking her all over – to see if she miaowed when something was painful – but that seemed a bit mean.

Then I wished I was psychic, so I could read Christine's catty mind. But even if I could, her thoughts wouldn't be in English, would they?

BLAM!

At that very second, I knew what I needed to do.

'Come here, puss,' I said softly, and scooped Christine cat into my arms.

Together we went pad-pad-padding down the stairs and into the kitchen, where Mum was pottering about.

'Er, what are you doing, Ruby?' Mum asked, raising her eyebrows at me.

'I . . . I just thought fresh air might make Christine feel better,' I replied, heading for the open back door.

'Well, I guess it might,' said Mum, smiling the sort of smile that told me she thought I was mad.

I felt her eyes following me as I wandered down the garden, but in a second I was safely out of sight, thanks to the giant rhododendron bush.

That's when I sped up, tippy-toeing to the low stone wall, where I sat myself and Christine cat down. With a swing of my legs

we were on the other side, and had entered
the hideaway world of trees, root tangles and
Thing.

'Hello!' I said softly to a dark doorway
hidden down amongst some leaves and
twigs. (Thing's den is an old Scooby Doo
Mystery Machine toy van that used to be
Jackson's.)

'Rubby!' Thing said happily, emerging

with one fat cheek and a half-eaten
mushroom in its paws. 'Wanting some?'

I shook my head.

'Chris-cat wanting some?'

'Thanks, but she's more into meaty
chunks,' I explained, as I sat down. 'And
anyway, I don't think she's very well today.'

'Oh! Is her *eyes* wrong? They very . . .
open!'

I understood why Thing would think that
was the problem. Christine normally had
her eyes firmly shut, dreaming happy old
cat dreams. Actually, the fact that she spent
ninety-nine per cent of her time sleeping was
also the reason Thing had never talked to
her in all the time we'd known each other.

But hopefully that was about to change.

'Thing, I was thinking . . . could you
maybe ask—'

We were interrupted by a scrabble and

a thunk, as Jackson vaulted over his high garden fence and joined us.

'What's up?' he asked, sitting down beside us on the scrubby ground.

'That's exactly what I want to find out,' I said, and turned back to Thing. 'Can you ask Christine if she's hurt?'

'Yes, *please*!' said Thing, waddling up to a miserable-looking Christine cat and gently stroking her paw with its own.

'Prrp? Mrrrrroaww?'

I felt Christine stir a little in my arms. Jackson scooted closer, keen – like me – to hear any response.

'Mrrrreww . . .' my cat feebly answered.

It didn't sound good, whatever it was.

'What did she say?' Jackson asked Thing.

Thing blinked its big eyes, racking its brain for the right words.

'Chris-cat feel . . . *blah.*'

'Blah? But what sort of blah?' I asked. 'In *pain* blah?'

'Not *paining*,' said Thing, with a scrunch of its nose. 'More like . . .'

Another silence. Another hunt in the head for the right word.

Except the silence was suddenly broken by a very particular sound.

'Blahhh-ahhh-ahhh-*urghhhhhh* . . .'

Christine retched in my arms – and coughed something completely unexpected right into Jackson's lap.

'What is *name* of that kind of blah, Rubby?' Thing asked politely, pointing to the odd, dry lump that looked like a cross between a cocktail sausage and a bit of bird nest.

'That's called sicking up a furball,' I told Thing matter-of-factly. 'Cats do it now and again.'

So *that* had been Christine's problem.

As for Jackson, he looked as horrified as he had done when the wood pigeon used him for target practice.

'Woof!'

That familiar, oh-so-close doggy hello made all of us jump – some more than others.

Feeling much better after her short barf,

an energised Christine leaped out of my arms and back over the wall.

And the close-at-hand scrabbling told me Thing was already halfway up the nearest tree.

'Frodo!' yelped Jackson, hastily brushing the furball out of his lap and jumping to his feet. 'What are *you* doing here again?'

But Frodo was more interested in whatever had just gone scampering into the branches above.

'Frightening Christine and Thing, *that's* what,' I told Jackson, as Frodo put his front paws on the trunk of the tree and barked.

'Eek!' squeaked Thing.

'C'mon, get down!' Jackson ordered Frodo. Frodo ignored him.

'Bark! Bark! Bark! Bark!!!'

'EEK!' Thing squeaked louder.

'Thing! It's all right!' I tried to reassure it.

'It *not* all right, Rubby!' Thing called down, rocking from side to side on its perch making all the nearby leaves shake like, well, *leaves*. 'Barker saying, "*Chase! Chase! Chase!*"'

'But it can't catch you all the way up there, Thing,' I pointed out.

Jackson, meanwhile, was feebly trying to grab hold of the dog's collar as it bounced round the trunk like a large, furry jumping bean.

'Whooo! Who-oooooo!' Frodo howled.

'AARGHH!' Thing yelped, slapping its tiny paws over its ears. '*No*, barker! I is not, not, *not* a SQUIRREL!!!'

Uh-oh.

Frodo hadn't just scared Thing – he'd deeply insulted it.

Thing *hated* squirrels.

And no wonder. Squirrels had never been very nice to it. I mean, would *you* like being

called a 'phlplplplpp'? (No, I don't know
what it means either, but apparently it's
very, *very* rude.)

'Hey! Here, doggy!' Jackson said urgently,
suddenly holding out a slightly fluffy and bent
jelly baby he must've found in his pocket.

Like me, he knew how dangerous the
situation was getting. A parent could hear.
Magic could happen.

Thank goodness Frodo wasn't put off by the jelly baby being a tiny bit grubby. He dropped on to all fours and sniffed the sweet in Jackson's hand.

Which gave Jackson the chance to grab hold of his collar so—

Uh-oh.

Out of the corner of my eye I saw something glitter.

Spling!

There it was again.

Spling! Spling!

Noooo! The jelly-baby distraction had come too late – the seriously spectacular weirdness had already started.

Thing's rubbish magic was in the air and there was nothing we could do to stop it.

Flickers of light danced round us, as if someone had set off a sparkler and that sparkler had gone cartwheeling off each of the five straggly trees.

Then, just as soon as this amazing mini fireworks show started, it stopped.

Rubbing the splings and sparkles from my eyes, I slowly opened them and dared myself to see what had happened.

Maybe Thing had turned the dog into a tree root?

Or a giant squirrel?

A massive, wobbly jelly baby, maybe?

Er, nope. None of those things had happened to Frodo. In fact, Frodo was nowhere to be seen. He'd disappeared. And so had Jackson. Where they had just been standing was now a giant pile of leaves.

'Thing . . . what did you do?' I asked.

'Um, not *know*, Rubby!' Thing purred nervously, peering down from the now-bare branch.

Ah, so *that* was it.

The tree Thing was perched in; it was suddenly naked. All of its greenery had fluttered into a mound on the ground.

A mound that was now shivering and shaking as two heads – one blond, one black and white – poked out of the top.

'What happened?' asked Jackson, holding on tight to Frodo's collar as the dog did a spin-cycle shake to rid itself of leaves.

'What do you *think* happened?' I replied, nodding up at Thing.

Thing was blinking its moon eyes in our direction.

'*Sorry*, Boy. *Sorry*, Rubby,' it purred in a tiny, shaky voice. 'But, Rubby – you take barker away now, yes, *please*?'

'Don't you want me to stay here with you?' I asked it. 'Jackson could take Frodo home, like last time.'

'No, thank you,' said Thing, ever so politely. 'Barker come *back*. Boy not do it right.'

Poor Jackson.

Of course I knew he was a useless donut.

But now even Thing had come to that conclusion.

It would be quite funny, if Jackson didn't look so hurt.

'Come on, we'll take Frodo back together,' I said, linking arms with my big, useless donut . . .

How to help a barker

'It's not *my* fault Frodo turned up again,' grumbled Jackson, as he plodded along the pavement next to me, holding on to his belt-lead.

What Jackson said was true.

The trouble was, he'd mumbled that same grumble about a zillion times as we headed off through the housing estate, towards Frodo's home.

'I mean, how can it be my fault if—'

'Is this it?' I deliberately interrupted.

We had just arrived in front of a house, which looked exactly the same as all the other new houses. All that made it different was the number on the door – 39.

I walked up the path and ding-donged the doorbell.

'Yeah. But Frodo just turning up like that; I couldn't help that, could I, Ru—'

'Shush! Someone's coming!' I told him, picking a stray leaf off his head.

Through the wavy frosted glass I could see the wibbly-wobbly outline of a woman and a skippy little kid looming towards us.

'Woof!' barked the dog as the door was pulled open.

'Frodo!' exclaimed a frazzled-looking woman with a paintbrush in her hand.

'Ha ha!' giggled a small, smiley girl,

clutching a doll with no head.

'It's not my fault!' said Jackson, as he unravelled his belt from Frodo's lead.

Not surprisingly, the frazzled-looking woman seemed a bit confused.

OK, it was time for *me* to talk, rather than the boy-shaped baboon by my side.

'Hello, I'm Ruby, Jackson's friend,' I said, introducing myself as Frodo galloped off into the house, followed by the skippy girl and her headless doll. 'Your dog got itself lost again. We found it over where we live.'

'Really? Oh dear . . .'

The frazzled-looking woman was obviously having a baby soon. (Any minute now, by the hugeness of her tummy.)

Wearily, she rested the hand with the paintbrush on her bump and ran her other hand through her tumbling-down, paint-splattered hair.

'I've been so busy getting the baby's room ready that I didn't even notice he was gone,' she sighed. 'How on earth did he get out? And why does he keep running away in the first place?'

'We could find out for you, if you like!' Jackson suddenly suggested.

'Sorry?' said the woman.

'We could find out why Frodo's running away!' Jackson carried on. 'Me and Ruby have this friend who can talk dog language.'

Noooooo! What was he *doing*? OK, so he wanted to help Frodo and his owner, but Jackson was in *serious* danger of splurging our small furry secret.

'You mean . . . like an animal behaviour expert?' asked the woman.

'Yes! Exactly!!' I practically shouted.

An animal behaviour expert sounded good. Sensible. Believable.

A tiny talking creature who lived at the bottom of the garden didn't.

'Well, that's very kind of you to offer,' said the woman, 'but I couldn't really afford it and I haven't the time to take Frodo *anywhere* at the moment. It's hard enough finding time to play with Posy.'

Posy . . . the smiley, skipping girl, I guessed. What a sweet name. And she had to be a pretty sweet kid; who else could love a doll with no head?

'Our friend would do it for free,' Jackson offered enthusiastically. 'And me and Ruby could take Frodo to see it right now!'

'"It"?' repeated the woman, crinkling up her nose.

'The animal behaviour expert, Jackson means,' I filled in quickly.

'Oh, that would be too much to ask of you . . .' said the woman.

'We don't mind,' Jackson replied. 'Do we, Ruby?'

Before I got the chance to say anything, the frazzled-looking woman sighed and said, 'Well, I suppose it couldn't do any harm!'

Oh yeah?

As the woman whistled for Frodo and

rootled round for a proper lead, I shot
Jackson a killer look.

His plan was all very well, but there was
one small hitch – a hitch called Thing.

How were we supposed to get it within
translating distance of the barker?

As if he could read my mind, Jackson gave
me a Cheshire cat grin and a big 'trust-me'
wink.

Ha!

The only thing I could trust Jackson
Miller to do was something completely
dumb . . .

Translating
with sausages

Amazingly, Jackson had a good idea. Honest.

In amongst the straggle of trees (and the giant mound of leaves), sat me, Frodo and a plastic carton of mini cocktail sausages.

A safe distance away, Thing tippetty-toed along a line – a line of jelly babies. Each one Thing came to, it stopped and ate it.

And with each stop, it warily eyed the dog.

'Barker *not* going to chasey-chasey, Rubby?' Thing asked, edging closer.

'I'm holding Frodo's collar really tightly,' I promised. 'And anyway, he's more interested in these sausages than you.'

I fed Frodo another one, just to prove my point. As he slobbered over my fingers I looked up and gave Jackson a hopeful smile.

Yes, the bribes of sausages and jelly babies had been his idea, amazingly.

'There. I just *here*,' Thing said suddenly, stopping dead with several jelly babies clutched to its chest. '*Not* nearerer barker.'

'OK,' Jackson agreed, sitting down cross-legged. 'And I'm right beside you if you get scared. Yeah?'

'Yes, *please*,' purred Thing, leaning up

against Jackson's bare knees. 'Now what is you wanting me to *say* to barker?'

'Can you ask Frodo why he keeps running away?' I told it.

Thing took a last bite of jelly baby, then made a funny 'huh-huh-hurr' noise.

At first I thought it was choking.

In fact, I was *just* about to order Jackson to turn Thing upside down and whack it on the back when I realised Frodo had – surprisingly – lost interest in the sausages.

'Huh-huh-huh-hurrr-huh,' panted the dog.

Ah! So *that's* what Thing and Frodo were doing – panting at each other!

Me and Jackson exchanged glances, as the breathy conversation continued.

Then – at last – it seemed to be over.

With one final pant, Frodo stuck his silly spaniel snout into the plastic carton of tiny sausages and ate the last ten in one huge, happy gulp.

'So, what did he say?' Jackson asked Thing.

'It say small human *mad*.'

'Small human?' Jackson frowned.

'Posy, I suppose?' I muttered, though I found it hard to picture that pretty, skippy little girl being *mad*.

'Small human sometimes put *nice* food in barker's mouth,' Thing carried on. 'Off her plate. Or from something called "bin".'

'Well, that doesn't sound very mad,' I said. Actually, it sounded like every dog's dream.

'But then small human also put *bad* stuff in barker's mouth.'

'Like?' said Jackson.

Thing blinked and wobbled, searching for unfamiliar words.

'Stuff called "perfume" and "toot-paste" and "*Lego*".'

Oh . . . so maybe Posy wasn't quite as sweet as her name.

'And small human do *bad* games.'

'What sort of bad games?' I asked, giving poor Frodo a cuddle, even though his breath was a bit meaty.

'Small human tie "lastic bandies" around tail till tail go numb–numb. What *lastic bandies*, Rubby?'

'Sort of stretchy bits of string, see?' I told Thing, pinging my hair bobble.

'Stretchy . . .' muttered Thing, practising another new word.

'Anything else?' Jackson asked.

'Yes, *please*. Barker say small human

break stuff called "toys" and "plants" and "remote control" and say, "Barker did it!"'.

'Maybe that's what happened to the doll's head?' I suggested to Jackson.

He shrugged a suppose-so back at me.

'Huh-huhhhh-hurrrr-a-hurr.'

Me, Jackson and Thing all turned to listen to what Frodo was now panting, though only one of us understood.

'Barker say small human also like to *lock* him.'

Me and Jackson frowned at Thing, while Thing frowned back, wondering how to make us understand.

'Lock barker in *room*,' it added. 'Lock barker in small space called "cupboard". Lock barker out of *home*.'

'So *Posy* is the one letting Frodo out of the house,' Jackson exclaimed. 'And then he just wanders off!'

'Well, that makes sense,' I agreed.

Posy was only little; she didn't realise how badly she was behaving.

And her mum had been too busy lately to notice what was going on.

'We'll go straight back round and tell Frodo's owner,' Jackson announced. 'Can you let Frodo know, Thing? Can you tell him everything will be all right?'

Thing nodded, then panted in the dog's direction.

But instead of panting back, there was a sudden explosion of barking.

Thing huddled in the baggy leg of

Jackson's shorts, its paws over its ears.

'Barker say "*Hurray! Hurray! Hurray!*", but too *loud*,' it squeaked.

'Bark! Bark! Bark! Bark! Bark! Bark!' Frodo carried on, excitedly.

'Shush, doggy!' I tried to quieten him, but it didn't do any good.

'Bark! Bark! Bark! Bark! Bark! Bark!'

AARGHH! If only pets had 'Off' buttons like Go Go Hamsters or Baby Annabels . . .

'Bark! Bark! Bark! Bark! Bark! Bark!'

'What's going on down here, eh? What's all this noise?'

EEK!

That deep, tall voice belonged to a man peering over Jackson's fence.

'Hello, Mr Miller,' I mumbled, remembering my manners, even though I was about to faint with panic.

'Uh, this is Frodo, Dad!' said Jackson, as he

shuffled a bundle of Thing further up the leg
of his shorts.

'What — the dog you were telling me
you found the other day?' Mr Miller asked
amiably. 'Don't tell me it's got itself lost
again!'

'Well, yeah,' Jackson shrugged. 'And me

and Ruby were trying to find out why it keeps running away.'

'Maybe it's because you're feeding it!' he said with a grin, nodding at the empty, family-sized carton of 'fifty cocktail sausages'.

'We, uh, just wanted to get its trust before we asked it what was wrong,' Jackson mumbled.

Mr Miller totally cracked up at that.

'You and Ruby are dog-whisperers now, are you?'

I'd heard that phrase on TV. People who had a way with animals were called horse-whisperers or dog-whisperers or whatever.

I guess you could do that for *any* creature.

Maybe not fish, though.

Being a fish-whisperer could be tricky. You might drown, for a start.

Still, me and Jackson didn't have a talent

like those whispery guys. But if it's what Mr Miller wanted to think, that was fine.

'We just wanted to help,' I told him, hoping I sounded honest and true, and not like someone who knew that his son was hiding a shocking secret up his shorts.

'Tell you what,' said Mr Miller. 'I'll get my shoes on and meet you round there in a minute. Then we can walk that runaway hound back home together.'

'OK, Dad!' Jackson said brightly, with his hand covering the strange-shaped bump on the side of his thigh.

Mr Miller turned to go, and my shoulders had only *just* started to sag with relief, when he swivelled round and peered over the fence again.

'Hey, I just noticed – what's going on there?' he asked, pointing to the nearly nude tree nestling shyly amongst the others.

'Freak tornado?' Jackson suggested.

He may be a donut, but at least Jackson made his dad laugh.

In fact, we heard his dad laughing all the way up their garden as he wandered safely away from us.

'Fnuffff!' snuffled Frodo.

'I know I don't speak dog,' I whispered to Jackson. 'But that sounded a lot like "Phew" to me!'

'No, *thank* you,' came a muffled, purry whisper from Jackson shorts. 'Barker just say "sausage!"'

I fondly ruffled Frodo's ears, wondering if I'd just found something with a smaller brain than Jackson's . . .

Walkies!

'Boing! Boing! Boing!'

'Shush, now, Posy – Mummy's talking.'

We were sitting in Frodo's living room;
that's me, Jackson, Mr Miller and Valerie
(Frodo's owner).

There were others in the room, only they
weren't sitting.

Frodo was lying on his back, tongue
hanging out, fast asleep after an exciting
time getting lost/found/translated/fed
cocktail sausages.

Posy was doing the opposite of sleeping; she was using an armchair as a trampoline and swinging her headless doll round by the leg.

There was *another* someone in the room, though only me and Jackson knew about that. Thing – and a few jelly babies – were nestled in the inside pocket of Jackson's jacket.

'Er, was that a good idea?' you might be
wondering to yourselves.

Probably not.

But while we'd waited by the trees for
Mr Miller to join us, Jackson had convinced
me that Thing should come along with us
to Walnut Grove, in case Frodo panted any
more important information.

To be honest – even though it was hidden

– I felt a *tiny* bit sick about taking Thing out into the big, wide world.

Then again, nothing TOO awful could happen in such a short space of time, so close to home.

Right?

(I crossed my fingers, which made it kind of hard to hold the biscuit and juice carton Valerie had just given me.)

'Boing! Boing! Boing!'

'Posy! Are you listening to me?' her mum sighed.

(Answer: no.)

'So,' Mr Miller carried on, in spite of the boinging, 'as I was saying, Valerie. there *was* no "animal behaviour expert"'. It was just two kids who were keen to help out.'

Mega-pink.

That was the shade of my cheeks, and Jackson's too.

The way Mr Miller was explaining the situation, me and Jackson sounded like silly three-year-olds.

'Boing! Boing! Boing!' yelled the ACTUAL silly three-year-old in the room.

'Well, I appreciate the thought,' said Valerie, smiling at us both.

She had a smudge of apple-green paint on her nose, I noticed.

'And we *did* find out what's happening,' Jackson announced.

'Oh yes?' said Valerie, with an I-don't-THINK-so raised eyebrow.

Jackson threw a quick look at Posy. But she seemed so caught up in her boinging and doll-swirling that she wasn't listening to what boring grown-ups and ten-year-olds were saying.

'It's *Posy* who's been letting Frodo out. She's been bugging him in lots of other ways too!'

'Now, Jackson's just *guessing* all this, Valerie,' Mr Miller jumped in.

'No, I'm n—' Jackson started to protest, till me and his dad shut him up. Me by glaring at him to keep our secret SECRET and Mr Miller by holding up a firm hand to him.

'But perhaps it's worth considering what Jackson's said,' Mr Miller continued. 'Young children *can* sometimes be a little rough with pets without realising what they're doing.'

'BOING! BOING! BOING!'

Valerie winced at the noise and eyed up her daughter.

'Hmm . . . well, Posy has been a bit *giddy* recently,' she said thoughtfully. 'I found her painting the toilet seat green just before you arrived. But I didn't think she'd be mean to Frodo.'

'BOING! BOING! BOING! Oops . . .'

Posy's headless doll went flying across the

living room. The *whack!* as it hit the far wall woke Frodo from his doggy dreams and made Jackson's jacket jump.

'I didn't do it!' Posy piped up, with a plastic doll leg still clutched in her hand. 'It was Frodo!'

Valerie narrowed her eyes at her daughter, as the truth became clear.

'Posy, come here,' she said, wiggling her finger.

Posy reluctantly jumped down on to the

floor and dragged herself over to the sofa, where her mum and Jackson were sitting.

'Now,' Valerie began, once Posy had plonked herself down between them. 'Have you been opening the front door and letting Frodo out?'

'No, Mummy.'

Posy innocently blink-blink-blinked her big blue eyes.

'So how do you think he's escaping, then?' Valerie asked her daughter.

'Maybe he's opening the door himself, because he wants to go out for a walk and a wee-wee?' Posy suggested hopefully.

'You know, Frodo really *isn't* getting enough exercise at the moment, but he'd have to be a very *special* sort of dog to unlock and open a door . . .'

'He *is*, Mummy, he really *is*,' Posy nodded at high speed.

'Hmm,' sighed Valerie. 'I think we'll talk about this with Daddy later. All right?'

'We should be going,' said Mr Miller, putting down his mug on the table.

I was just about to do the same with my juice carton when a thought pinged into my head.

'Mrs . . . Valerie?' I said shyly. 'If you're very busy just now, painting and, er, having a baby and everything, maybe me and Jackson could take Frodo out for a walk sometimes?'

Valerie's eyes lit up as if I'd given her the best Christmas present ever.

'Oh, that would be lovely! Did you hear that, Posy?'

But Posy wasn't paying attention to her mum any more. She was busy staring at Jackson. From the fear in his eyes, you could tell she was freaking him out. Maybe she was imagining him headless, like her doll.

'Posy – Ruby and Jackson have offered to take Frodo for a walk now and again.'

'Ooh, can *I* go too?' Posy asked, her eyes still fixed on poor Jackson.

What? No way! I didn't mind hanging out with an overexcited dog, but I didn't fancy being in charge of a wild animal like Posy.

'I don't think so, darling,' Valerie said, much to my relief. 'Now, do you want to show our visitors out?'

With a bunch of smiles and final chit-chat, me, Jackson and Mr Miller stepped through the front door. Jackson in particular looked relieved to be getting away from the intense glare of the small human.

'Now what do we say, Posy?' Valerie prompted her daughter.

I think Frodo's owner was hoping for a polite 'thank you for coming', or 'thank you for bringing our dog back'.

Instead, Posy opened her rosebud mouth and said, 'That boy's jacket was making *eating* noises!'

Help . . . she must have heard Thing nibbling its stash of jelly babies!

Luckily – going by this afternoon's revelations – the grown-ups seemed to have decided that everything Posy said was a great, fat, kiddy fib.

And so they just laughed, laughed, laughed.

'A jacket making eating noises!' Mr Miller repeated, as we tootled off along Walnut Grove. 'Can you believe it?'

'No,' me and Jackson said in unison.

Though I knew we were both thinking 'Yes!' with knobs on . . .

A snuggly white lie

'Hungry?' asked Mum, picking a pot off the cooker.

'Definitely, Mrs Morgan!' Jackson answered enthusiastically.

'Well, I'm glad my spaghetti bolognese tempted you to come inside,' she added, now pouring the steaming ribbons of pasta into a colander by the sink. 'I think you two would stay out by those trees all day if you could!'

Ding-doinggg!!

'*I'll* get it,' I called out to Mum, since she had her hands full with boiling water and squiggly pasta.

Screeching back the chair, I hurried to open our front door.

'Hello!' said a man on the doorstep. 'You must be Ruby.'

'Uh, yes . . .'

The man knew who *I* was, but I didn't have a clue who *he* was.

'And are you Jackson?' he added, looking over my shoulder.

'Yeah!' said Jackson, shuffling up to my side.

'Can I help?' Mum's voice breezed down the hall — and then there were *three* of us staring at this stranger in a suit.

He suddenly seemed to realise he should
explain himself.

'I'm Paul Thomson.'

Nope, that didn't help.

'Posy's dad? Frodo's owner?' he tried
again.

'Ah . . . !' we all sighed together.

'I just wanted to say a big thank you,
Ruby, Jackson, for all your help with Frodo.'

'That's OK,' Jackson answered for both
of us.

'You guys certainly solved the mystery of how Frodo kept "escaping" – Posy's finally admitted she was locking him out of the house,' said Mr Thomson. 'In fact, Posy told us some of the other "funny" things she's done to Frodo while our backs have been turned. We'll be keeping an eye on that now!'

As Frodo would say, 'Hurray!'

'Now Valerie and I have been thinking of a way to thank you properly, and actually *Posy* helped us come up with something.'

'There's really no need—' Mum began on our behalf, but Mr Thomson stopped her with a wave of his hand. A hand holding an envelope.

'Not at all. It's a pleasure,' he insisted. 'Anyway, Posy was telling me about the little creature she saw peeking out of your jacket the other day, Jackson – hamster was it? Or a guinea pig?'

Nooooo!

When we'd dropped off Frodo, Posy hadn't just *heard* Thing munching on jelly babies; she'd *spotted* it too!

'What's this?' asked Mum, smiling expectantly at Jackson.

Jackson opened and shut his mouth, like a goldfish caught in the headlights.

Yikes.

I had to get us out of this mess.

Brain – give me a good excuse, and *quick*.

BLAM!

OK, I'd got one.

The only problem was, Jackson wasn't going to think it was any good.

'It's a toy – it wasn't real,' I blurted out. 'It's Jackson's, um, "snuggly". He can't sleep without it, and carries it around with him sometimes. But he doesn't like people to know.'

Jackson went so red from my embarrassing white lie that I could practically feel the heat scorching me.

'Aw,' murmured Mum, patting Jackson on the shoulder.

'No worries, mate, won't go any further,' Mr Thomson said reassuringly. 'But with your kindness to Frodo and your, er, toy guinea pig, we reckoned you were both animal fans. So Valerie and I thought you'd like these.'

I took the envelope Mr Thomson was holding out, peeked inside, and spotted three tickets.

HAPPY VALLEY PETTING ZOO GALA DAY! was printed on them.

'We *were* going to take Posy, but her granny's coming for a visit,' Mr Thomson continued. 'Do you know the Petting Zoo?'

I nodded my head – last time I was there was for a classmate's eighth birthday party.

Jackson shook his head – I keep forgetting he only moved round here pretty recently.

I'd describe Happy Valley to him later. With 'Zoo' in the title, he might be expecting lions and tigers and boa constrictors. But it was more of a farm really, with sheep and bunnies and ducks. The cool thing was you could stroke them and feed them carrots and stuff, which was fun. (And you can't do *that* with lions and tigers and boa constrictors, can you? If you like your arms, I mean.)

'They're for this Saturday,' said Mr Thomson, pointing to the tickets. 'It's a special Gala Day, so there are going to be fairground rides and a parade.'

'How lovely!' Mum exclaimed. 'Well, I'll talk to Jackson's parents, but I'd certainly be happy to take these two along.'

As Mr Thomson turned and headed for his car, Mum gasped, and hurried back to the bolognese sauce she'd left cooking. Or maybe *burning*.

'That was great, the way you covered up for Thing,' Jackson said quietly to me, while we smiled and waved at Mr Thomson.

'Thanks,' I whispered back.

'But, Ruby,' he added, still smiling, still waving. 'Telling your mum and Mr Thomson I have a "snuggly" . . . you *do* realise I'm going to have to kill you for that?'

Well, it was fair enough, really.

And luckily for me, Jackson'd planned on *tickling* me to death.

'Noooooo!' I squealed, running away from his wibbly fingers as fast as I could . . .

Pop! goes the bubblegum

'... *And* there'll be geese,' I could hear Jackson say, as I got down to the bottom of the garden.

'What is *geese*?' asked a familiar little voice.

'Birds.'

'*Birdies* . . .' Thing repeated. Sort of. 'I *like* pretty little birdies. What *elses*?'

'Rabbits. And hamsters. And guinea pigs.'

'I *knows* rabbits. But what *hammies* and *giggly pigs*?'

'Uh, imagine rabbits, but a bit smaller, with no ears,' I heard Jackson answer uselessly, as I clambered over the wall.

'Well, hello!' I said, landing on the other side.

I'd expected to see Jackson and Thing, but not Frodo. From my first, quick glance, I noticed that the dog was happily eating a stick to bits, and didn't seem at *all* interested in chase-chase-chasing Thing.

And hey, Thing didn't look too freak-freak-freaked by Frodo being so close.

Since their panting session a couple of days ago, they seemed to have bonded, I was pleased to see.

'Rubby!' Thing squeaked with delight, as if it hadn't seen me since at least yesterday. 'Where is you *been*?'

I guess it *was* quite late (quarter to five), but me and Dad had stuff to do after school.

'I went for a check-up at the dentist.'

Thing blinked.

I realised that I might as well have said, 'I went for a be-doink at the flubber-doodle.'

'A dentist is someone who looks at your teeth, and makes sure they are healthy and strong,' I told it.

'*Healthy* and *stroing* . . .' Thing repeated, biting its diddy teeth together. 'These *good* stuff, Rubby?'

'Yes,' I replied, settling down beside Frodo and giving his ears a scratch. 'It's important to have healthy, strong teeth.'

'*And* a healthy, strong body!' Jackson joined in, putting his arms up and flexing his invisible muscles.

'*Stroing* good,' muttered Thing, copying Jackson's pose and looking adorably silly.

I was about to mention the importance of
a balanced diet too (we did it as our topic
at school this term) but explaining stuff to
Thing can sometimes be as tricky as eating
jelly with chopsticks.

And anyway, Thing wouldn't really *get*
what a balanced diet meant, since all it eats
are mushrooms, mushrooms and mushrooms.
Plus jelly babies, of course.

Speaking of jelly babies, I needed to ask the King of Jelly Babies a question.

'Jackson, did Frodo find his own way here again?' I asked, imagining Posy shoving him outside with the leg of her headless doll.

'Nah . . . I went round earlier and offered to walk him, and—'

'*Grrrrrrrrrrr.*'

We both whipped our heads round and saw Thing doing something it shouldn't.

I mean, it didn't seem like a FANTASTIC idea to go lifting up Frodo's lip and staring into his mouth.

'Look, even *I* know that Frodo is saying "leave me alone"!' I said to Thing.

Thing instantly jumped away from Frodo, letting his lip drop like a rubbery curtain.

'I only look there to see if barker is *stroing* and *healthy*, Rubby! And he *not* say "leave me alone". He say "this stick *mine*!".'

'Well, whatever Frodo said, I'd like you two to stay friends, so please stop playing with his teeth,' I told Thing.

Then I remembered I had a second question for Jackson.

'Hey, what were you and Thing talking about when I got here? I heard you mentioning animals.'

Jackson looked up from something he was unwrapping.

'I was just telling Thing what it would see at the Happy Valley Petting Zoo tomorrow,' he answered, chucking some gum in his mouth. 'Want some?'

'What? *No!*' I yelped, swatting away the gum he was offering. 'Jackson, we are *not* taking Thing to the Petting Zoo. It isn't safe. Thing could get discovered! What if someone sees it? Like Posy the other day! What if it does magic? We could get in terrible trouble – *again*!'

While I ranted and fretted and jabbered, Jackson slowly blew a huge pink bubble, watched by a fascinated Thing.

'Have you been listening to a word I've said?' I asked, realising I sounded a lot like Posy's mum all of a sudden.

POP! went the huge pink bubble.

'You basically said no, Ruby,' he mumbled, slurping the gum back into his mouth. (Urgh, gross!)

'Well, that's because it's a really *terrible*

idea,' I said as I watched Jackson offer a piece of gum to Thing.

'Boy, how I get big pink *ball*?' it asked.

'You just put it in your mouth and blow,' Jackson instructed.

'Jackson!' I snapped. 'We are *not* doing this!'

POOT!

That was the tiny sound of Thing putting the bubblegum in its mouth and blowing it straight back out whole, without realising you were meant to *chew* it first.

GULP!

And *that* was the

sound of Frodo lunging over and swallowing the small, hard square of gum whole.

Good grief . . .

Between them, Jackson, Thing and Frodo had all the common sense of a very small pebble.

In fact, I'd probably be better off talking to the half-chewed bit of stick lying discarded in front of Frodo.

'*ROOOOBBBYYY! TEA'S READY!*' Mum's voice drifted from the back door of our house.

'I've got to go,' I muttered, getting to my feet. 'But Jackson – you have to *promise* me, hand on heart, that we are *not* taking Thing with us tomorrow.'

'I promise, hand on heart,' Jackson replied,

clutching his fists to his chest.

It wasn't till halfway through my pudding that I realised what he'd done. I let out a long, low groan.

'Ruby, are you OK?' asked my mum.

'Excuse me!' I said, pretending it had been a weird-sounding burp instead.

But of *course* it had been a most definite oh-no, I-can-never-trust-that-boy groan.

Cos your heart's on the left, isn't it?

And Jackson – the big, sneaky donut – had his hands clutched to the *right* side of his chest.

Great.

So I guessed Thing – all giddy and overexcited about seeing hammies and giggly pigs – WOULD be coming with us on our trip tomorrow . . .

Down a dead end

'Woof!' said the dog standing at the entrance to the Happy Valley Petting Zoo.

Then it handed me a leaflet.

Because *this* dog was actually a spotty-faced teenage boy in a fancy-dress outfit.

And the leaflet he'd handed me described what was going to be happening at the Gala Day today:

DONKEY RIDES!
SHEEP RACING!
BALLOON ANIMALS!
MAIZE MAZE!
PET PARADE!
FAIRGROUND ATTRACTIONS!

I passed the leaflet over to Jackson. While he read it, I glanced round and saw . . .

• a busy farmyard, packed with kids and their grown-ups, all oohing and aahing, eating ice cream and candy floss.

• barns and fences and outbuildings covered with rainbow-coloured bunting.

• a paddock with donkeys that had flowers entwined in their bridles.

• another paddock, where a whole fun
fair was crammed in.

'So!' my mum said brightly. 'What's first?
Deadly Dodgems? Octopus of Terror? Or the
Cuddle Barn?'

'Octopus of Terror!' said Jackson.

'Cuddle Barn!' said me.

'What?' Mum laughed. 'Ruby, I know you
like animals, but you LOVE fairground rides.
I thought you'd have been desperate to get
on the Octopus!'

I do love fairground rides.

And I **WAS** desperate to get on the
Octopus of Terror.

But one thing was stopping me.

Or should I say, one *Thing*.

Cos our weird woodland pet has a habit
of getting travel sick. It could just about
cope with car journeys, but I think its tiny
tummy might have a very big problem with
a ride that whizzed round and round at
high speed.

'Maybe later,' I said, shrugging.

'Go on, Ruby!' Jackson pleaded, not thinking for a second about our stowaway.

'Well, if *I* was you two, I'd take your chance now,' said Mum. 'Look – the ride is slowing down, and there's hardly a queue at the moment. It could get really busy later.'

Mum had her hand on my back, gently pushing me towards the fun-fair field.

I muttered a few more 'I don't really want to's but Mum kept laughing, thinking I was joking, and of course Jackson didn't help.

'Aw, come on, Ruby!' he urged, as we got right up to the barrier.

Fine, I thought, as Mum handed some money to a guy selling ride tickets. *Thing is in Jackson's bag. So HE'LL have to clear up the mess if it gets ill . . .*

A second later I was sitting in a pod of an octopus tentacle with Jackson clambering in beside me.

But uh-oh – something was wrong.

Jackson had been grinning like a big baboon, but now he looked as sick as a Thing on a rollercoaster.

'What?' I asked, as the octopus began to move.

'Your mum . . .' he mumbled. 'She said, "Here, *I'll* take that for you"!'

'Take what for you?' I asked urgently.

SWIRL!

Just then, as we began to circle off, I spotted Mum. She was waving with one hand – and holding Jackson's backpack in the other.

'You left Thing with my mother?!' I yelped, as we wheeled out of view.

'I couldn't help it! She grabbed the bag off

my shoulder before I could stop her!'

SWIRL!

'Well, I suppose it'll be all right,' I said,
trying not to panic as we zoomed by my
waving mum again. 'Thing will just stay still
and the ride will be over in a minute.'

SWIRL!

'Aargh!' groaned Jackson, spotting Mum
on the third whirl. 'She's just dumped the bag
down!'

'Ouch!' I winced, imagining Thing being

thunked and clunked on to the ground.

SWIRL!

'Noooo!' I gasped on the fourth whirl.
Now Mum had picked up the bag and was
opening it!!

SWIRL!

'What's she looking in my bag for?'
Jackson yelped on the fifth whirl.

'I don't know, but she's going to find Thing
— that's for sure!'

SWIRL!

On the sixth whirl, the ride slowed to
a stop and we warily stepped out of the
octopus.

I'd expected to see my mum screaming or
white-faced with shock.

Instead, the bag was back on her shoulder
and she was smiling cheerfully at us.

'I have an apology to make to you,
Jackson,' she said, as we got closer.

'Uh, yeah?' he replied in a teeny-weeny voice.

'I popped your bag down on the ground, and heard a funny *squeaky* sort of noise. I was scared I'd broken something; your mobile or DSi maybe, so I had a quick check.'

Her face had gone all squishy, like grown-ups do when they see a cute baby or whatever.

'And I spotted you'd brought your snuggly along,' she said with a sympathetic tilt of the head. 'But don't worry – your secret's safe with me!'

Ha! Mum had no idea just *what* kind of secret she'd actually seen.

But what were we going to do? We had a whole afternoon together, me, Jackson, Mum and Thing. It was only the first five minutes and I was already stressed out. I'd pass out with panic if this went on.

'By the way, guys,' Mum added. 'Can I ask you a favour? I'm dying for a cup of tea. How about you two leave me in the café and have a wander round on your own?'

You have never heard a boy and a girl yell 'YES!' more loudly.

'Oh, well, great!' said Mum, reeling from our enthusiasm. 'Maybe meet me back here in half an hour? And while you're away I can look after your bag, Jackson . . .'

You have never heard a boy and a girl yell 'NO!' more loudly.

'Thank goodness for that . . .' I sighed, as Mum finally walked off in search of tea and cake.

'We should go somewhere quiet and check on Thing,' Jackson suggested, gently cradling his backpack.

'But where?' I asked, glancing round and seeing . . .

- crowds 'n' queues for the donkey rides
- crowds 'n' queues for the fun fair
- crowds 'n' queues for the ice-cream van and candy-floss twirler
- crowds 'n' queues for the man bending and boinging balloons into funny animals.

RIDES

And although I couldn't see inside the Cuddle Barn, I knew there'd be crowds 'n' queues galore, waiting their turn to hold and stroke small, furry somethings.

Where on earth could we safely hold and stroke our *own* small, furry something?

'*I* know!' said Jackson, pointing to a signpost for the Maize Maze. 'Follow me!'

After a few minutes of weaving, bobbing, 'excuse me's' and zigzags, we gladly found ourselves in a dead end.

Here and there we could make out giggles and shouts of 'This way!' and 'Help!' but the voices were JUST far enough away to make us feel safe.

'Come on out!' I said softly to Thing, unsnapping the clip and unzipping the zip of Jackson's bag.

'Are you OK?' asked Jackson, as I cradled the woozy bundle of big-eyed red fur in my arms.

'My head, it not feel very *healthy* and *stroing*,' Thing purred, rubbing a spot behind its pointy left ear.

'Oh, poor you!' I said. 'But you did brilliantly, Thing. You must have been so scared when my mum peeked in the bag.'

'Mmm,' Thing agreed. 'I stay very, *very* still.

I stay, very, very, very, very, *very* still. It hard when mum lady do *this* to my tummy.'

Thing wiggled the little pads in its paws And giggled. (In case you want to know, the sound of Thing giggling is a lot like a kitten sneezing.)

'She tickled you?' asked Jackson.

Huh? Why would Mum 'tickle' Jackson's 'snuggly'?

'Mum lady say in small voice, "Where *squeaker*?",' said Thing. 'What *squeaker* is, Rubby?'

'Ah, she thought you were a toy, with something inside you that made a noise.'

Thing experimentally pressed its tummy and we all undoubtedly heard a tiny noise – a miniature rumble.

'Have you brought any jelly babies?' I asked Jackson. Since there was no way to find an ice pack for Thing's bumped head in the middle of a Maize Maze, I thought the next best thing for Thing was to distract it with food.

'Sure! Red, green, yellow?' he suggested, holding a few up.

'Yes, *please*, thank you,' replied Thing, grabbing them all.

Phew. I could see it perking up nicely with every squidgy bite.

Its moon eyes were taking in the straw-yellow 'walls' around us and its squirrelly ears were gently revolving, listening to the trills and yelps going on nearby.

'What *is* here, Rubby?' it suddenly asked.

'We're in a Maize Maze!' Jackson answered instead, holding up the map he'd grabbed from a different teenager, this time in a panda outfit, on the way into the maze.

'*Maisie-zizz-zizz*?' Thing blinked, its tiny tongue vibrating.

'Maize is a big plant, and you can eat *these* parts,' I explained, pointing to a ripening corn on the cob amongst the leafiness. 'And the Petting Zoo has turned this field of maize into a maze.'

'Which is all twisty and turny and people can get lost in it, which is a lot of fun!' Jackson added enthusiastically.

'Why lost is *fun*, Boy? Lost *sad*!'

Thing blinked fast. It must be remembering the bad old days of the chainsaws and shrinking forest. The days it had to scurry to ever-shrinking chunks of the woods that it had never been to before.

'Look, I'm guessing that you promised to take Thing along today so it could see all the animals, right?' I said to Jackson.

Jackson and Thing both nodded.

'So how about we get out of here and head to the Cuddle Barn?'

'Good idea,' nodded Jackson, holding up the Maize Maze map and studying it.

Then turning it round and staring hard.

Then swivelling it upside down and biting his lip.

Then giving it another quarter turn and looking worried.

'Don't you know how to get out of here?' I asked him, alarmed.

'It's a bit confusing, that's all,' Jackson mumbled. 'I mean, if I just knew where the wooden lookout tower was then I'd know where we were . . .'

Our time was valuable. It would only be so long before Mum finished her tea/cake/relax and started angsting about us being late back to meet her.

'Thing – if I hold you up so you can see over the top of the maize, can you tell us where the tower is?' I asked, raising it high before it had a chance to answer.

'Yes, please, Rubby. I do that for you – EEK!'

WHUMF!

I brought Thing straight back down.

'What? What did you see?' I asked.

'A floaty pink bubble, like one *Boy* blew in mouth,' Thing babbled. 'But this made of *longness*, not *roundness*. And it have a face!'

A bubblegum bubble that was long with a face?! What was Thing on about?

'A balloon animal! Bet *that's* what it was! Didn't you see the guy making pink pigs?'

Jackson said very surely. 'Hey, Thing — you
know Ruby's swimming cap?'

Thing nodded. It loved the lookalike
trampoline we'd made for it out of my old
cap and a cake tin.

'Well, that's made of something called
rubber. So are balloons. Balloons come
very small, but if you blow air into them
— like bubblegum — they get bigger and
bigger!'

'Oooh!' Thing cooed, rubbing its paws together. 'I see *again*, Rubby?'

'OK, I sighed, holding it up once more. 'But don't forget to tell us where the wooden tower is so we can—'

'EEK!'

I brought Thing straight back down again.

'Small boy human – it sit on head of *big* human, and see me!' it babbled.

But it wasn't just Thing's babbles we could hear. Over the wall of corn a kid's voice was yelping, 'Daddy! Someone has stolen a hamster from the Cuddle Barn! I just *saw* it!'

Noooo!

We had to get out of here, and fast, before me and Jackson got reported as pet thieves and Thing panicked and magicked us into mayhem.

'What shall we do?' I fretted at my large two-legged friend, as I bundled our little four-legged friend into the safety of the rucksack.

Jackson – amazingly – suggested some magic of his own.

'We walk through walls,' he announced, and disappeared before my very eyes . . .

10

Sparkles and sneets

If you try to walk through a brick wall, two things will happen . . .

1. You will get hurt, and

2. You will feel stupid.

But if you try to walk through a wall made of maize, *these* two things will happen . . .

1. You will find it a bit rustly and scratchy, and

2. You will find yourself easily on the other side.

So that's what we did, me and Jackson. Walked though about twenty leafy walls, popping out of the maze with only a few light scratches and two big sighs of relief.

And now here we were in the cavernous

Cuddle Barn, home to tons of small furries, plus a few roaming geese and pot-bellied pigs.

To be exact, we were huddled in a corner, me, Jackson and the backpack. The backpack was turned so its small mesh air panel faced out. That way, Thing – snuggled safe and unseen inside – got a great view of all the animals.

It also had a great view of the gazillions of kids all squiggling impatiently on benches, waiting their turn for a hamster or gerbil or

guinea pig to cuddle.

But suddenly an announcement blasted over the speakers, making everyone – and everything – in the Cuddle Barn jump.

'The Sheep Race is about to finish, folks, and will be followed in a couple of minutes by the Grand Pet Parade!'

'What *is* a Sheep Race and a Pet Parade?' Jackson asked me.

I remembered the petting zoo's Sheep Race from the time I came for my classmates' birthday. Happy Valley staff hung numbers round all the sheeps' necks then sent them running round a course.

As for the Gala Day Pet Parade, I had no idea. Was everyone meant to grab an animal and conga along, cheering?

'So anyone who wants to catch the Pet Parade, please make your way to the Farm Yard now!' the announcement continued.

There was major scuffling as kids with laps full of pets hurried to hand them back to the Cuddle Barn staff and run outside.

'Nah,' me and Jackson agreed together, knowing the Pet Parade crowd would be no fun for an easily squashable Thing in a bag. We'd stay right here.

'HONK!' a wandering goose called out, finding itself shooed out of the way by stampeding kids.

'Rubby,' I heard a voice purr softly.

No one was within hearing distance of our corner, but to be on the safe side, I bent over and pretended to tie my shoelace.

Seeing what I was doing, Jackson did the same. The big donut.

'Yes?' I whispered to the bag, trying to ignore my copycat friend.

'These *birdies* . . . not *like* normal birdies,' Thing said from the depths of the backpack.

'Very, *very* big. Very, very, very, very, *very* big!'

'Well, technically, they're geese,' I replied.

'Peh! Birdies *sing* pretty. *Big* birdie geeses not sing pretty. They have sore throatie?'

'HONK!' the same grouchy goose called out at a snuffling, skedaddling, pot-bellied piglet.

'And this giggly pig,' Thing murmured, 'it swallow beach ball, I think?'

'Er, no,' Jackson said with a grin. 'It's *meant* to be that shape. And that's actually *not* a guinea pig. A guinea pig is much small—'

'Here, sonny, do you want a turn?' said a woman who was wearing a T-shirt with Happy Valley Happy Helper! on the front, and holding a snuffling furry bundle in her hands. 'This little darling is called Delilah.'

And that's how Jackson ended up with a puzzled-looking guinea pig sitting in his lap.

'Sneet!' Delilah squeaked, as Jackson

stroked her. 'Sneet! Sneet!'

I glanced up, and saw that the Barn was emptying fast. Nearly all the kids and parents had gone to watch the Pet Parade, leaving just three Happy Helpers to pop the various furballs back into their cages.

'Thing,' I said softly to the bag. 'What does "sneet" mean?'

Well, I was curious, wasn't I?

Before Thing could answer, a bellowing from the speakers interrupted us.

'*Announcement: could we have all staff to the Farm Yard, please? Sheep numbers 6, 9 and 15 have escaped and are running amongst the Pet Parade.*'

With that, the Happy Helpers scampered out of the Barn, completely forgetting that one of their furries was still with us.

Excellent.

Now I could whip open the zip and let

Thing scurry out and talk directly to that furry.

'Not speak giggly pig, but will *try*,' said Thing.

'Sneet! Sneet-sneety-sneet–sneet!'

While Delilah sneeted away in Jackson's lap, Thing studied her intensely.

'It say—'

'Hey, what exactly's going on outside?' muttered Jackson, all of a sudden grabbing up the left-behind Delilah and turning to stare out of the window at the noise and bustle out there. 'You know, looks like the Pet Parade is just a bunch of those teenagers in fancy dress, dancing badly to "Hakuna Matata" from *The Lion King*. With sheep.'

Jackson made it sound pretty funny, but I couldn't concentrate.

Mainly because I could feel a familiar trembling going on.

'Thing . . . what's wrong?' I asked quickly.

'Rubby, giggly pig saying all day small humans squishy and squash her. Giggly pig grumpy!'

Thing was rocking from side to side, rubbing its paws madly.

'I *worry*, Rubby. Small humans maybe *break* giggly pigs and hammies and germbles?'

'No, I think they'll be OK, real—'

'But they giggly pigs and hammies and germbles so *small*!' Thing fretted on, feeling more trembly by the second. 'Not *healthy* and *stroing*. If they bigger it better!'

I tried stroking Thing, hoping I might calm it (and knowing I wouldn't).

'Yes, but—'

Spling!

Uh-oh.

Spling! Spling!

Amongst the snuffly furries and sawdust, the sparkles twinkled.

Yep, the seriously spectacular weirdness had already started.

Spling! Spling! Spling!

CRACKLE SPIT FIZZZZzzZ!!

Thing's rubbish magic was filling the Cuddle Barn, and there was nothing we could do to stop it.

Flickers of light danced round us, as if someone had set off a sparkler, and that sparkler had gone cartwheeling off amongst the hutches and runs and roof beams.

Then, just as soon as this amazing mini fireworks show started, it stopped.

'Thing?'

But I didn't need to ask what it had done.

Thing's tiny mind had been filled with bubblegum and balloons lately, and it showed.

Rising out of Jackson's arms was a great fat furry guinea pig, expanding by the second.

At first Delilah was the size of . . .

- a melon,
- then a football,
- then a pumpkin,
- then the exercise ball that my mum uses for her Pilates class.

'Sneet!' squeaked Delilah, as she rose higher and higher the rounder and rounder she became.

And it was about to get worse.

'Ruby – look over there!' Jackson called out, pointing to the hutches and runs.

Help . . .

All of the hamsters and gerbils and guinea pigs were starting to expand too. They looked a little like floating, furry Christmas tree baubles.

'Thing!' I said, turning my attention to the creature sitting in my lap. 'Turn them back *now*, before someone comes in and sees this!'

But as usual, Thing didn't know how to reverse its rubbish magic.

And it would have been too late, even if it did – because someone *had* just walked in.

'Excuse me – anyone seen any sheep in here?' asked the giant squirrel.

'EE–'

I slapped a hand over Thing's mouth but heard the rest of the 'K!' on my palm.

I could also – GULP! – feel the vibrations beginning again.

'Nope! *No* sheep here,' said Jackson.

Amazingly, the giant squirrel (and the teenage girl inside the costume) turned and hurried out, without noticing the giant expanding guinea pig bobbing above her head.

'Didn't she *see*?' I said incredulously.

'Not with that animal head on,' Jackson answered. 'She could only peek out through those tiny eyeholes. Which is lucky for— Oh no! What's happening *now*?'

Pop!

The shock of seeing a squirrel – a really *huge* squirrel – had given Thing the heebie-jeebies.

PoP! POP!

The seriously spectacular weirdness had started *again*.

PoP! PoP! PoP!
cRACKLE
sPiT
FIZzZZzzZ!!

Flickers of light, sparklers, cartwheels . . . the whole works.

As I watched the mini fireworks show slow to a stop, I realised I'd had my fingers crossed so tight they'd gone white.

But suddenly it seemed that the squirrel-stress had been worthwhile.

Cos there in Jackson's arms was a normal, guinea-pig-sized guinea pig.

And in the hutches and pens, average-looking, non-floaty furries were sneeting and squeaking.

I can't pretend to know what rodents are chatting about, but I bet right now it was something to do with the heaps of jelly babies piled up in all their food bowls.

'Er . . . what's with the jelly babies?' I asked Thing.

'They *nice* food,' it purred nervously. 'Make hammies and giggly pigs and germbles *healthy* and *stroing*. Yes, *please*, Rubby?'

I didn't answer, cos right at that second, Delilah gave an extra-loud 'sneet!'

'What did she say?' I asked Thing.

'She say sorry,' it purred, blinking up at me with don't-be-cross eyes.

'Sorry for what?' I asked, frowning.

'Urghhh . . .' groaned Jackson, holding Delilah away from him and studying the warm, damp patch that had leaked on to his cool T-shirt.

'Ah, here you are,' came a familiar, lovely voice at the door.

'Mum!' I called out, sweeping Thing into Jackson's backpack. 'Is it still mayhem out there?'

'Yes – but the runaway sheep have been caught by a teenage tiger, cow and meerkat, so it's settling down. Hey, isn't it nice and quiet in here?'

'Fnurghhhhh!'

Poor Mum.

She must've thought me and Jackson had gone loop-de-loop crazy crackers.

And we kept laughing *all* the way home in the car . . .

Happy ending(ing)s

Boo!

There – *that* got your attention again.

Just thought you might have wandered off to get a drink or a snack or something, thinking my story was over.

But it isn't quite.

Yes, it's been fun to tell you about Jackson being pooed, furballed and weed on.

But the fun doesn't stop there, oh no.

'Can you believe it?' said Jackson the other day, as we mooched at our straggle of trees.

'What — that you have a brain?' I suggested. 'Well, it *is* quite hard to believe, I guess.'

'No!' Jackson answered with a frown. 'Can you believe that Frodo's owners have named their baby after *me*?'

'I know,' I said, more seriously. 'But

SNIFF-
SNIFF-

personally, I think it's kind of cruel to call a kid "Donut" . . .'

I got a handful of leaves in the face for that (no surprise).

Jackson grabbed them from the pile that had unexpectedly – OK, magically – fallen off the tree the week before.

Frodo was snuffling round the pile, pretending he was a tip-top sniffer dog, instead of a perfectly dopey pup.

'Ha ha!' Jackson said sarcastically in my direction.

But my baboon of a buddy really was hugely chuffed that Valerie and Paul Thomson had decided to call their brand-new baby boy Jackson after him, because they liked the name so much.

Or maybe it was because it was just cos he'd offered to look after Frodo for a few days, till they got themselves 'sorted out'.

(Don't know what 'sorting out' is needed when you have a baby, but in Frodo's owner's case I thought it *might* mean getting a muzzle for Posy.)

'BOO!' yelped Thing, bursting out of the leaf mound and frightening the life out of Frodo.

CLAMP! went Jackson's hand over the dog's mouth, before he began barking the place down again.

'Ha! I do *funny* thing to barker, Rubby!' Thing announced as it rustled over to my lap.

'Well, I'm just glad you two are friends now,' I replied with a smile. 'That's a really happy ending.'

'What is *happy endinging*, Rubby?' Thing asked, gazing moonily up at me.

I could've told the truth, of course. But I was suddenly in the mood for a lie.

'It's *this*!'

I grabbed Thing – and blew a giant raspberry on its tummy, making it giggle and giggle like a sneezy kitten.

So, did you like my story, and its tickly happy ending(ing)?

Maybe you'd like to hear another.

I'm sure there'll be one right along soon.

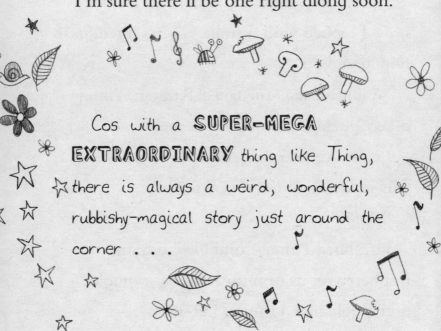

Cos with a **SUPER-MEGA EXTRAORDINARY** thing like Thing, there is always a weird, wonderful, rubbishy-magical story just around the corner . . .

Beware of the Snowblobs!

YOU, me
and
Thing

Contents

A sighing sort of noise

'Peh!'

That little noise was made by my very small friend.

My very small *furry* friend.

No, it's not a pet. Not exactly.

And it's not a person, though it *does* talk.

My very small friend is . . . well, a thing, called Thing.

Thing used to live deep, deep in the dark, dark woods behind my cottage. But there *are* no dark, dark woods to live deep, deep in any more. Not since a big, ugly new housing estate was built in its place.

When that happened, Thing scuttled to the safety of the straggle of trees just behind my garden. And that's where me and my neighbour (and friend and idiot) Jackson found it.

Thing's been our fuzzy, talking, magical secret ever since.

'Peh!'

Thing makes that little noise whenever it's fed up. I guess 'peh!' is Thing-speak for 'sigh'.

Jackson hadn't noticed the peh-ing

❋ FOREST VIEW ESTATE ❋

because he was too busy tossing jelly babies
in the air and catching them in his mouth.

Hurray! One missed, hit him in the eye
and bounced on to the hard, scrubby ground.

'Are you OK?' I asked.

'No, not really. Ouch,' said Jackson,
covering his injured eye with his hand.

'I wasn't talking to *you*,' I replied, with my
gaze turned on Thing.

The three of us were hunkered down by
the tree roots, with my garden
wall and Jackson's tall fence

sheltering us from our parents' view.

Jackson's mum and dad and mine; they think we have a den. They think it's cute that me and Jackson spend lots of time here after school and at the weekends.

They might be just a *teeny* bit completely shocked if they knew we were not alone.

And just a *weeny* bit totally alarmed to know we were best buddies with a weird, winged, talking creature.

'*Not* OK, Rubby,' mumbled Thing, in its funny, purry voice.

'*Ruby,*' I gently corrected it.

Which was a waste of time, since Thing never gets my name right. And it can't even *remember* Jackson's name.

'What's bothering you?' I carried on.

I wondered if Thing was fed up because I'd just told it that soon we wouldn't be able to come and visit after school, as it was getting dark really early cos of winter.

But nope; it wasn't that.

'This mess very *wrong*,' it said, pointing to a nearby knobbly tree root. Or at least something that was growing on it.

'You mean *moss*?' I checked, leaning over to peer at the bright-green fuzz.

'Yes, *please*.' Thing nodded.

'What's wrong with it? Wrong colour? Do you fancy some *purple* moss? Or red? Tartan, maybe?!?' Jackson joked uselessly.

Thing looked up at him with its huge moon eyes and then turned to me.

'What Boy is *saying*, Rubby?' it asked.

'Ignore him,' I told Thing. 'Now what exactly is the problem?'

Thing rocked a little from side to side, rubbing its paws together.

'When time for *cold* is coming, I make nice, cosy, crunchy beddy,' it explained.

Er, I didn't exactly understand its explanation. Still, like Jackson, I turned to look at the mound of assorted twiglets and ferns that hid Jackson's once-upon-a-time-favourite toy.

The toy was an old Scooby Doo Mystery Machine van, which had turned out to be the perfect home for a homeless Thing.

Here's a very short list of stuff that Thing kept inside the van:

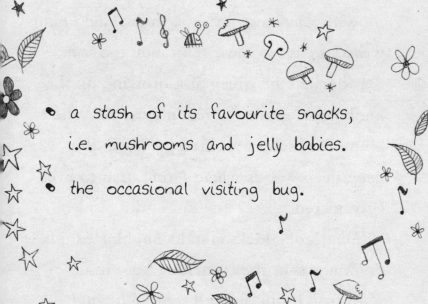

- a stash of its favourite snacks, i.e. mushrooms and jelly babies.
- the occasional visiting bug.

(*Told* you it was a short list.)

But, yes, winter was definitely on the way. The sky was packed full of fat grey clouds, the wind was sharp and whippy, and the end of Jackson's nose was red and slightly dripping (yuck).

So I could see that Thing might want to make its nest a little more snuggly.

'How do you make a cosy, crunchy bed, then?' I asked.

'With *right* mess, not *wrong* mess,' said Thing, wrinkling its wee nose. 'This mess too *softie*.'

I touched the green fuzz growing on the knobbly tree root – it really was soft. What kind of crunchy moss had grown in the deep, deep woods where Thing used to live? I wondered.

'Hey, look!' Jackson suddenly blurted out, pointing up at the branches above us.

At first, I thought he'd spotted a patch

of Extremely Rare Crunchy Moss growing higher up in the trees.

Then I saw the wonderful twirls of white spiralling down . . .

'Wow!' I exclaimed, smiling at the sight of snowflakes big as cornflakes.

'Brilliant!' yelped Jackson. 'My cousins and my nan are coming this weekend. Me and Matt and Luke are going to have the BEST fun with snowballs!'

'*Snow*blobs, *snow*blobs, *snow*blobs . . .' muttered Thing, practising this new word.

'And we can go sledging too!' said Jackson

'What is *sludging*, please?' Thing asked, its squirrelly ears and flightless, stubby wings twitching with interest.

'Something you absolutely HAVE to do, Thing!'

'It's something Thing's NEVER going to do, Jackson,' I burst in. 'You know it's not safe to take it out where people might see it!'

'Sludging is *good*?' Thing asked Jackson eagerly, ignoring me and my sensible words as much as Jackson was.

'It is SO good!' said Jackson, holding his jelly-baby packet out so Thing could help itself. 'A sledge is this flat chunk of plastic that you sit on and then you ZOOM down a hill very fast!'

'Oooh!' purred Thing, entranced.

I knew Thing hadn't a clue what plastic was.

Or a hill, for that matter.

What I *did* know was Jackson + Thing + snow equalled trouble for sure . . .

Projects and snowpigs

'It's going to be great, isn't it?'

I wasn't talking about the snow.

Though it *was* great.

Since the flakes began fluttering yesterday,
the world had got itself whiter and whiter.

In fact, the playground at school today
had a perfect padding of whiteness – till
breaktime, when everyone tore outside and
went nuts stamping all over it, scooping up

snowballs or shaping snowmen.

Or snow*dogs*, if you were Jackson.

'*Isn't* it going to be great?' I said again, as I drew my name in the snow with the toe of my wellie.

'Mmm,' mumbled Jackson, concentrating on his snowdog.

It was supposed to look like Frodo, our neighbours' bouncy spaniel, which we sometimes take for a walk. If I was a mean person (I'm not) I'd have pointed out that it looked more like a lumpy snow*pig*.

'I can't wait, can you?' I tried once more.

'Mmm,' Jackson grunted.

When Thing says 'peh!', it means 'sigh', right?

Well, when Jackson says 'mmm', I know it means 'I'm only *pretending* to listen to you, Ruby.'

Grrr . . .

'So, how about that alien standing right behind you, saying he's going to eat your brain?' I asked, as a test.

'Mmm.'

Of course no alien would *want* to eat Jackson's brain (it would probably give them a tummy upset, or even just terrible wind).

But I *had* proved that my donut of a friend wasn't paying attention to me *at all*.

'Jackson!' I said loudly, crouching down beside him and his snowpig. 'Don't you think it's great that we're having an art day tomorrow?'

This morning, Miss Wilson our teacher

told us about the different types of celebrations people hold in winter, like Christmas (for Christians) and Diwali (for Hindus) and Hannukah (for Jews). From tomorrow, we'd get a chance to make all sorts of celebration decorations. It was going to be brilliant fun.

'Huh? *What* art day?' grunted Jackson, his blond eyebrows bumping together in a frown.

'Uh, *hello*?' I said, crouching down beside him and waving a hand in front of his face. 'Weren't you listening to *anything* Miss Wilson was saying in class?'

'Nope,' said Jackson. 'I was thinking about my cousins coming tomorrow night. Luke and Matt are *so* cool. Did I tell you about the time Matt ate cat food for a bet? And that Luke can burp any song you ask him to?'

Yes, Jackson had told me that already.

He'd also told me that Luke was the same age as us and Matt was three years older.

And I knew that Matt broke his arm last summer when he skateboarded into a post box and that Luke nearly drowned when he dive-bombed into a river dressed as Spider-Man, aged three.

Jackson might be a donut, but his cousins sounded like they were *dangerous* donuts.

'I can't *wait* to have a snowball fight with Lukey and Mattster!'

I shuddered at what Jackson just said.

His cousins' nicknames weren't the problem.

And neither was the snow.

I mean, I love snow.

I love snowmen.

But I *hate* snowballs.

That's why I was glad Jackson had decided to make his snowpig over near the dinner hut, which was pretty far from where most of today's playground snowball battles were happening.

'What's wrong?' asked Jackson, suddenly noticing my shudder.

'When I was in Year 1,' I began, 'Shaun Robertson hit me on the back of the head with a really icy, hard snowball.'

'Ouch,' said Jackson.

'Exactly!' I nodded. 'I sat all through afternoon lessons feeling dizzy. And the snowball was wedged in my ponytail, so it melted really, *really* slowly down my back and . . .'

It was bad enough when Jackson was 'mmm'ing at me.

But now he did something *much* worse.

In the middle of what I was saying, he bolted upright, completely ignoring me!

'Hey, that's ru—'

I didn't get to the 'de' part.

I was too busy watching Jackson jump in *slooooowwwww motionnnnnn* and **THWACK!** he expertly caught a speeding snowball in mid-air.

WOW.

If Jackson hadn't leaped to my rescue, it

would've clonked me *right* in the face.

'Thanks, Jackson,' I said, all stunned and grateful. 'You're my hero!'

Jackson blushed pink to the roots of his blond hair.

'S'all right,' he mumbled shyly.

'And aww, look! Catching that made you squash your snowpi— I mean, snowdog!'

I pointed at the stomped-on mound of snow under his wellies.

'Doesn't matter,' said Jackson, shrugging off his good deed and squished snow sculpture.

I do moan about Jackson.

Especially when he acts like a big baboon and suggests dumb stuff like smuggling Thing into the outside world.

But y'know, when he tries, he can be a really, truly, *excellent* best friend.

'Hey, Ruby,' he said now, tossing the

snowball up and down in his hand.

'Uh-huh?' I smiled.

'I was thinking – *can* we take Thing sledging? My dad's got this big, floppy hat with flaps that I could wear, and if Thing maybe lies *flat* on my head and peeks out under the front . . .'

As Jackson wiggled the fingers of one hand near his forehead, I stared down at the other, which was still holding the snowball.

Now, if I slipped my hand underneath . . .

Just one *quick* flick upwards . . .

It was so tempting.

I shouldn't do it.

Will I?

Won't I?

SPLAT!

'Hey, what was *that* for?' Jackson spluttered through a mouthful of snow.

'Because you should *know* why we can't

take Thing sledging!' I said. 'And if you don't,
then your squished snowpig is smarter than
you, Jackson Miller!'

'Yeah? Well, at least *I* can spell my name,
Ruby Morgan!'

I turned to look where snow-faced
Jackson was pointing, and saw the letters I'd
absentmindedly scraped with the toe of my
wellie.

They spelt 'RUBBY'.

'I *meant* to do that,' I lied, then stepped
over the squished snowpig and stomped off
in a huff.

SPLAT!

I think that MIGHT have been a handful of snowpig landing in the middle of my back.

But maybe, just this once, I deserved it…

The sound of schlumfing

Whatever Dad was cooking for tea smelled good.

And more importantly, it smelled nearly ready.

Uh-oh – I'd have to be QUICK.

'Where are you going, Ruby?' asked Dad, as I flipped up my hood and headed for the back door.

'Um . . . just down to the trees,' I replied,

hoping he wouldn't ask what the bulge in my skirt pocket was.

'But it's dark out there,' he said, peering out of the kitchen window.

True. While Mum and me had been at the shops after school, the sun had tipped right off the edge of the sky.

'It's OK, I have *this*!' I said, smiling brightly and waving the pumpkin-shaped torch I got for trick or treating at Halloween. 'I just want to see how pretty the garden looks in the snow!'

Dad rolled his eyes, but gave a 'whatever' shrug. 'You've got five minutes, Ruby. All right?'

'All right!' I answered, pulling the back door closed behind me.

SCHLUMF! SCHLUMF! SCHLUMF!

(That's the sound of running through deep snow in your wellies.)

SWOOSH! THUMPFF.

(That was me jumping over the low stone wall at the bottom of the garden and landing on the other side.)

'Oh!'

(That was me being surprised at finding myself alone.)

Where was Jackson? I supposed he'd already been and gone while I was at the shops with Mum.

I shone my pumpkin on the ground, but didn't spot any boy-shaped footprints.

Crouching down, I peered under the tangle of twigs and ferns and saw that the back doors of the Mystery Machine van were closed.

I could hear the faint sound of rustling and 'peh!'ing coming from inside.

'Thing?' I said, with a tippety-tap on the plastic, just to be polite.

'Rubby!'

The doors were flung open, and there was Thing, holding a large dry leaf in one paw – with more bits of dry leaf stuck to its fur here and there (and everywhere).

'What have you been doing?' I asked, reaching over and brushing its tummy clean with my hand.

'I try to make *nice* beddy, but this all too crunchy,' it purred, tossing the leaf to one side.

'Ah! Well, I brought you this – I thought it might be just what you needed!'

I pulled the squidgy something out of my skirt pocket and held it out.

It was a sponge.

Not the *foam* sort; this was one of those holey, knobbly-bobbly sponges that once upon a time were living things in the sea.

I'd spotted it in the supermarket and thought it might make PERFECT nesting material for Thing. (Mum was surprised that I wanted it, but I said I'd pay for it out of my pocket money.)

'*What* it?' asked Thing, poking the sponge with its finger.

'Here,' I began, tearing a chunk off. 'Maybe it's a little bit like your favourite moss? It's kind of cosy *and* crunchy . . .'

Thing squidged the piece of sponge in its paws.

Then squidged it some more.

Then *WHOOSH*! the whole of the sponge vanished from my hand, as it – and Thing – disappeared inside the van.

'Fnah . . .'

Rustle, rustle.

'Tfffff . . .'

Scuffle, scuffle.

'Erk!'

While Thing worked on remodelling its den, I busied myself with building the world's smallest snowman.

It was tiddly enough to have an acorn shell as a hat and eyes made from two crumbs from my jacket pocket (there was a half-eaten flapjack in there, kept for emergencies).

'*What* it, please, Rubby?' I heard Thing suddenly ask.

It was hunkered in the doorway of the

van, holding a large chunk of sponge in one paw – with more bits of sponge stuck to its fur here and there (and everywhere).

'A snowman,' I explained, once again reaching over and brushing its tummy clean with my hand. 'Kids – and sometimes grown-ups too – make them for fun.'

'A *snowmum* . . .' Thing repeated thoughtfully (and wrongly).

'No, it's not a snow*mum*. They're supposed to look like *people*, so they're called sn—'

'Snow *peoples*,' Thing purred, interrupting me (and getting it wrong again). 'I *like* little tiny snow peop—'

'BARK! BARK! BARK! BARK! BARK! BARK!'

'It *Dog!*' chirped Thing, recognising

Frodo's woofing. 'It say "TREES! FRIENDS! PLAY! TREES! FRIENDS! PLAY!"'

Uh-oh.

Sometimes Frodo escapes from his house on the estate when his family isn't looking. Or when the owner's three-year-old daughter Posy thinks it would be fun to lock her pet out of the house. Had that happened again?

Er, no.

'Thing? Ruby? You there?' I heard Jackson call out, as he and Frodo wriggled and scrabbled through shrubbery from the Willow Avenue side of the trees.

'Oh. Did you take Frodo out for a walk after school?' I asked, surprised.

Jackson hadn't mentioned he'd planned on doing that.

Mind you, we'd been in a huff with each other all day and not really talking.

Jackson was huffy with me for saying the

snowpig was smarter than him.

And *I* was huffy with Jackson cos he threw a second snowball at me at break, which went sloshing into my wellie and left me with an all-day soggy sock.

'Well, I went round to ask Mrs Thomson if I could take Frodo along when I go sledging in the park with my cousins this weekend,' he said, 'and Frodo got *so* excited when he saw me that I HAD to take him for a quick walk round the blo—'

'EEEEK! Not *do* that, Dog!!!'

At Thing's panicked squeak I shone the pumpkin on the ground.

The mini snowman was melting . . . melting under the stream of wee that Frodo was widdling all over it.

'Stop! No!' I yelped, trying to shoo the dog away.

Frodo, thinking this was an excellent

game, started barking and bounding about on the spot.

Help . . .

Frodo's woofs would get Dad's attention for sure.

But that wasn't the *main* problem. In the beam of the pumpkin I spotted Thing rocking back and forth, obviously upset at seeing the little snowman vanishing. And when Thing gets upset, strange stuff tends to happen.

Strange MAGICAL stuff.

(Don't go thinking that's good – it's not, trust me.)

And we couldn't risk Dad or anyone *else* getting a glimpse of random, strange, magical stuff, could we?

'Jackson!' I said urgently, as I dropped the torch and grabbed Thing with both hands.

'Hello?'

Hello?!

THAT wasn't what I was expecting Jackson to say! I'd thought he'd blurt out 'What are we going to do, Ruby?' or 'How do we get Thing to stop?'.

I peered in the gloom and saw that he had his mobile wedged to his head.

'Oh, hi, Luke! Yeah! I know!

Brilliant!' Jackson twittered, talking on his phone. Had someone called him, and I hadn't noticed, what with all the squeaking (Thing), yelping (me) and barking (Frodo)?

'Jackson!' I hissed urgently, feeling Thing trembling against my chest. We were seconds away from all sorts of crackles, fizzles, magic and muddles.

'Yeah! Definitely! It's going to be totally *ace*!!'

'JACKSON!!' I hissed louder, frantically stroking Thing in the hope that it might calm it down.

'What? No way! Ha ha ha ha ha . . . !'

Worry fluttered in my chest like a butterfly gone bonkers.

'RUBYYYY! TEA'S READY!' Dad's voice drifted down the garden.

No!

What was I going to do?

Thing was about to turn the snowflakes into baked beans or the bits of sponge into luminous jellyfish or do some *other* rubbish magic that would get us all found out and—

'Hee hee!' came a teeny-tiny giggle.

Oh.

I felt Thing's trembling begin to ease.

Phew – the magic had stopped before it got a chance to start.

And what had made that happen?

Not me and my frantic stroking.

Not anything Jackson had said or done, since he was *still* babbling on the phone to one of his cousins.

'Hee hee! Stop! Oooh!'

The magic had fizzled away thanks to *Frodo*.

'Good boy!' I whispered, as the dopey dog carried on licking Thing all over – *and* my fingers too (bleurgh).

Maybe all the licketty-licking was Frodo's way of saying sorry to Thing for weeing on the snowman.

Or maybe he just thought Thing tasted nice.

Whichever, it had tickled Thing out of its panic, and got us all out of a truckload of trouble.

All the while, Jackson - the big donut -hadn't even *noticed* …

'COMING, DAD!' I yelled, as I gently popped Thing on to the ground and scooped up my pumpkin.

Pausing only long enough to blind Jackson with a beam from the torch ('Ow! What did you do *that* for?'), I jumped over the wall and *SCHLUMF! SCHLUMF! SCHLUMF*ed my way home for tea …

4

From a woof to a WHATEVER . . .

I had two plans for Friday . . .

1. I was going to have fun making celebration decorations in class.

2. I was going to stay mad at Jackson all day.

But by ten past nine he'd made me laugh *so* much Miss Wilson gave me one of her Scary Starey Teacher Looks.

It was cos of Jackson's goofy-but-great impression of Frodo.

Whenever Miss Wilson turned away to demonstrate one of the crafts, Jackson pulled on the flappy-eared hat he'd borrowed from his dad, flopped out his tongue and turned into a dog.

And he carried on making me laugh all day, by refusing to talk and only *bark* what he wanted to say.

(Well, not in class. When he tried it with Miss Wilson, she glowered so hard at him that he whimpered, I swear.)

'Arf! Arf!' he barked

now, lolloping about as we walked out into the playground at the end of the day.

'Jackson, stop it!' I giggled. 'Stop trying to lick my face — that's disgusting!'

Jackson suddenly stopped.

Jackson suddenly went bright red.

Jackson suddenly yanked off his mad, flappy-eared hat.

Huh?

After a whole day of puppying about, he seemed awkward, or embarrassed, or something.

What had changed?

'OI! PEANUT!' came a roar.

'LUKIE! MATTSTER!' Jackson roared back, and then hurtled away from me towards the school gate.

There, waiting for him, was Jackson's mum. Which was no surprise, as it was her turn to pick us up.

Beside her was an older lady. (Jackson's nan, I guessed.)

And with them were two boys – his cousins, right? – who immediately JUMPED on Jackson – and started punching him!

'HEY, PEANUT!' roared one of the boys.

'Peanut'? That was their nickname for Jackson? I'd have to ask him later how it had come about.

'YAY, LUKIE!!' Jackson answered the

smaller of the two boys.

'RAAA! C'MERE!' yelled the one who
had to be Matt, now getting Jackson in a
headlock.

While the three boys wrestled, shouted
and hurt each other, Mrs Miller and
Jackson's nan beamed at them, as if they
were as adorable as kittens.

'WHAT'RE YOU DOING HERE?'
Jackson asked, bent double. 'THOUGHT

YOU WEREN'T COMING TILL TONIGHT!'

'We wanted to surprise you, sweetheart!' said his nan, gently tugging at Matt's arm to let his cousin go.

'C'MON!' said the one who was Luke, slapping an arm round Jackson's shoulders. 'LET'S GO BACK TO YOURS!'

'COOL!' roared Jackson, beginning to lurch off.

'Er, Jackson . . . haven't you forgotten someone?' Mrs Miller pointed out.

Jackson looked at one cousin, then another, then looked confused.

'I meant *Ruby*!' his mum said with a smile. 'Aren't you going to introduce her to everyone?'

'Uh, yeah, sure,' said Jackson, running a hand through his spike of blond hair. 'Ruby, this is Nan 'n' Luke 'n' Matt.'

Weird.

Weird for *two* reasons.

1. My funny, babbling idiot of a best friend sounded instantly different – sort of BORED.

2. Jackson, Luke and Matt – it was like looking at three versions of the same person, only in one of those mirror arcades at a funfair.

'WHO'S *SHE*, PEANUT? YOUR *GIRLFRIEND*?' said Luke, who was a smaller, slightly chunkier version of Jackson.

'FNAAH-HA-HA-HA!!!' said Matt, who was a super-scrawny, taller version of him.

I felt my cheeks go pink, pink, pink.

Jackson's did ditto.

'No *way*!' he replied, sounding disgusted. 'She's just some neighbour.'

Huh! What a cheek!!

'AND WHAT'S THAT? WHY'S SHE HOLDING A BLOB OF MUD IN HER HAND?' shouted the one who was Luke.

'It's *not* a blob of mud!' I mumbled. 'It's an art project.'

This morning in class, we'd made Christmas 'bells' out of the dome-shaped bits of egg boxes, and cut up kitchen roll holders to make the row of eight candles for Hannukah.

This afternoon, we'd shaped clay to make little candleholders called 'diva lamps' for Diwali. I hadn't had time to decorate my

diva lamp, so Miss
Wilson let me take
it home to paint.
(I hadn't had
time cos somehow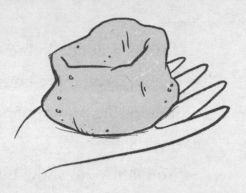
Jackson got clay in his hair and I had to
wash it out before it set rock hard.)

As I clutched my lumpy diva lamp, Luke
stared at me, as if he didn't understand what
I'd just said or even what I *was*.

Then he turned to Jackson and said,
'RACE YOU!' before legging it away from
the school gates.

Jackson and Matt zoomed after him.

'So, Ruby, I've heard *all* about you,' said
Jackson's nan, as we followed the boys.

I smiled shyly, only half-listening, since the
other half of me was busy being irritated by
Jackson and his drongo cousins.

'You two have a den, I hear?'

'Mmm.' I nodded absent-mindedly, watching as all three boys dashed on to the zebra crossing and disappeared round the corner.

'You'll have to show Luke and Matt your den – I'm sure they'll love it!'

Uh-oh. I heard THAT all right.

And now *I* wanted to be the one running.

I wanted to run *all* the way home to let Thing know it was in DANGER!

Hurry up and hide

Had my pumpkin turned into a carriage
and driven off somewhere?

Probably not.

But I couldn't find it anywhere.

I looked under the bed.

I looked under the wardrobe.

I looked under the pile of clothes that I
was going to tidy away (last Thursday).

I even looked under Christine cat, but

there was no sign of my pumpkin-shaped Halloween torch.

It was only dusk outside, but that meant it would be gloomy down by the trees, and I *had* to search for any signs of Thing that needed to be hidden.

For a minute or two, my mind stayed in a muddle.

Then – *ping*! – an idea appeared as if a lightbulb had been switched on.

Or a Diwali candle had been lit . . .

'Mum?' I said, finding her in the kitchen. 'Do we have a tealight for my diva lamp?'

'I think we might have one in here . . .' she replied, rifling in the cupboard.

'Can I film it?' I asked, once she'd lit the candle for me and stuck the matches back in the drawer.

'If you like!' she laughed, passing me her phone.

Mum obviously thought I was a tiny bit mad.

She had no idea that I was *actually* being very sensible.

Here's why . . .

SCHLUMF! *SCHLUMF*! *SCHLUMF*! went my wellies in the snow, just a little while later.

'Thing?' I called softly, slipping myself over the low wall at the bottom of the garden.

I could hear faint rustling, and definite 'peh!'ing.

'Rubby!' Thing purred.

I held up Mum's mobile. In the soft glow of the tealight, I could see that Thing was trying to shove what looked like several empty jelly-baby packets into the back of the Mystery Machine van.

Yes — the soft glow of the tealight that I'd *videoed*. How much safer was that than carrying a real – and really dangerous – lit candle round with me?

'Are you using *those* for your winter bed?' I asked, crouching down beside Thing. I could now make out tossed-aside bits of sponge near the outside of the van doors.

'Mmm, sponge too *sproingy*, so I *try* these,' muttered Thing, sounding uncertain. 'But what is little shaky light, *please*, Rubby?'

Of course, living its whole life deep in the heart of a forest, Thing wasn't going know too much about fire.

'It's a sort of moving photo of something called a *flame*,' I explained, trying not to snigger as Thing sniffed at the screen, and gave it a quick lick.

Then a sudden bellow of boy laughter from the direction of Jackson's kitchen reminded me why I was there.

'Thing, I have to warn you – Jackson's

cousins have arrived, and I think they might
come exploring down here.'

Thing's eyes widened in alarm.

'But Boy not *let* them, Rubby!' it
squeaked. 'Boy my friend – Boy keep me all
safe and secret, yes, *please*?'

'Well, Jackson would *want* to keep you
safe, Thing, but his cousins seem . . .'

Words rattled round my frazzled brain.

I didn't really know them properly, so how

could I describe Luke and Matt? What was the missing word? Crazy? Wild? Horrible?

'. . . boisterous,' I settled on.

'Boy– boys– boys *trees* . . .' Thing tried to repeat, rocking anxiously from side to side. 'What that *is*, Rubby?'

'Well, if they wanted to do something, I don't think Jackson would be able to stop them,' I said in as calm a voice as I could manage. 'But look, it'll be OK.'

'*How* it be OK, Rubby?' Thing squeaked again, rubbing its tiny paws together now.

'Well, first, we hide anything to do with you,' I replied, scanning the phone about and spotting that the snow was doing a good job of covering up the trampoline we'd made for Thing out of a cake tin and an old swimming cap.

Any stray jelly-baby packets were gone; stuffed into the back of the Mystery

Machine. All I had to tidy up were rejected chunks of sponge.

And Thing's one decoration – a small, laminated photo of a tamarind monkey – was easy to pull from the twig it was hanging from.

'Keep that here for now,' I said, reaching over and sliding it into the van. 'And MOST importantly, the *minute* you hear anyone next door coming out into the garden, hurry up a tree and hide there till they're gone.'

'Yes, *please*, Rubby,' said Thing with a solemn nod. 'I hide up tree till cuzzles all gone.'

'Just . . . beware.'

'I bees *wear*,' repeated Thing, nodding some more.

I squinted at it for any worrying signs of panic, EEEK-ness or any wobbles of

AARGHH!, but Thing seemed reassured by my plan.

'I'm going to have to go in now, Thing. But before I do, is there anything you want to ask?' I checked, not wanting it to worry about Jackson's dorky cousins.

'Before you going*ing*, Rubby,' it began, looking up at me with its big, trusting moon eyes, 'can you make me *nuther* little snow peoples?'

Well, how could I say no?

Handing the phone to Thing, I showed it how to angle the 'flame' so I could see what I was doing.

Then just as I began to scoop a body together, a *CRASH*, *BANG*, *WALLOP* and 'WAAAAAAHHHHH!' interrupted my snow-sculpting.

'YOU ARE *SO* GONNA GET IT, PEANUT!' someone roared, as a bundle of boys tumbled into next-door's garden.

'AIM FOR HIS *FACE*, LUKEY!' came a more muffled roar, like someone was trying to shout with a mouth full of pizza.

'TWO AGAINST ONE? NO' FAIR, MATTSTER!' I heard Jackson's voice call out, followed by some thuds and splats. 'OW! AH! OUCH!!'

'Rubby! Is cuzzles *hurting* Boy?!' squeaked Thing.

'Don't worry,' I hissed. 'I know it sounds like they're killing him, but it's just the way boys play. Pass me back the phone and hurry up the tree – you'll be out of sight

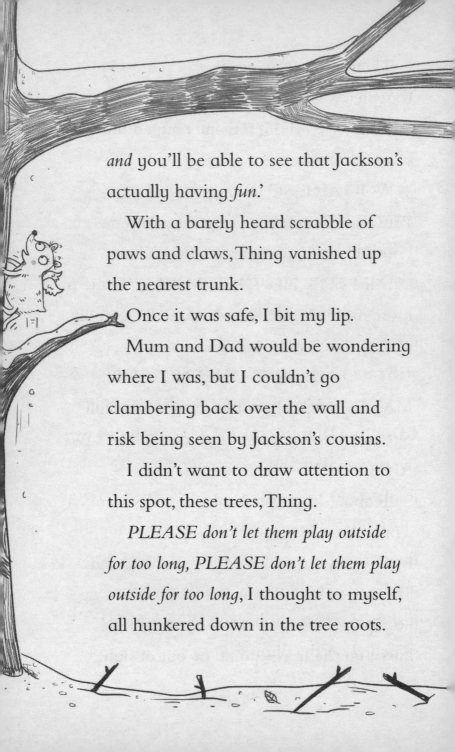

and you'll be able to see that Jackson's actually having *fun.*'

With a barely heard scrabble of paws and claws, Thing vanished up the nearest trunk.

Once it was safe, I bit my lip.

Mum and Dad would be wondering where I was, but I couldn't go clambering back over the wall and risk being seen by Jackson's cousins.

I didn't want to draw attention to this spot, these trees, Thing.

PLEASE don't let them play outside for too long, PLEASE don't let them play outside for too long, I thought to myself, all hunkered down in the tree roots.

Yikes!

There was a pair of hands in gloves, scooping snow off the top of Jackson's fence . . .

Stay still, stay silent; the boys are having WAY too good a time beating each other with snowballs to bother peeking over here, I thought some more.

Except – except a *head* was now appearing over the top of the fence.

A head that belonged to Matt, the skinny, tall cousin.

And – help! – he was staring *straight at me* . . .

'HEY, PEANUT! THAT NEIGHBOUR GIRL IS HIDING OVER HERE,' he shouted to Jackson, sounding a little bit freaked out.

AARGH – how could he have seen me in the dark?

Oh, the tiny flame of the diva lamp; *that* must've caught his eye. Why hadn't I switched off the phone?

'Uh . . . just ignore her,' I heard Jackson
say quickly. 'She's not worth bothering
about. Everyone round here knows she is
well weird.'

Excuse me?!?

Out of the two of us, I was *not* the weird
one. I mean, *who* acted like a dopey dog all
of today? Hmm?

But hold on; maybe Jackson just *said* that

mean-sounding stuff to get Matt to leave me
– and Thing – alone.

'HUH,' grunted Matt, thankfully
disappearing.

Yay! It worked!

As quick as I could, I slipped over the wall
and *SCHLUMF*ed up the garden.

Thanks to Jackson's fib, Luke and Matt
would think their cousin was living next to a
total dingbat.

And horrible as it was to hear your best
friend say mean-sounding stuff about you,
I was happy to act as mad as the maddest
dingbat if it kept our little Thing safe.

Cos Jackson was only pretending, wasn't
he?

(*Wasn't* he?)

Huffing and puffing

How do you make snowflakes flutter in a row?

Easily, if you're Miss Wilson.

Yesterday, when we were busy with our celebration decorations, she'd folded a sheet of white paper till it was small, small, small.

Then she snip, snip, snipped while we watched and wondered.

'Voilà!' she'd called out in French, un-folding the paper and showing off a pretty chain of snow-white snowflakes.

We all had a go, though our Christmassy paper chains looked more like wobbly triangles with holes than Miss Wilson's perfect patterns.

But hers had looked so lovely that I was determined to try again.

And this time I was folding up a white plastic bag I'd got out of the recycling box in the kitchen.

I was going to make some mini, outdoor, *waterproof* bunting, specially for Thing. I'd string it up between two twiglets, and Thing could lie cosy in its crunchy bed and stare dreamily at the snowflakes, even once the *real* snow had melted away.

Course, I wasn't going to hang it till Jackson's donut cousins had finally left.

I just needed to concentrate and cut very carefully right—

Tippetty-tap!

SNIP.

Startled by the sudden, small knocking sound, I cut *right* through a chunk of rustly plastic bag. Throwing the scissors and, er, not-quite-bunting on to the floor, I stared at my bedroom window.

'Rubby!' purred Thing, jumping up and down to attract my attention. I leaped up and tugged the window open.

'Hurry up and come inside!' I told it, scared that it might be seen.

Thing plopped down on to the floor, and blinked up at me.

'What are you doing here?' I asked, half listening out for footsteps on the landing.

'Last night I dreaming*ing* about movie photo,' it said. 'I *like* to see shaky light again, please?'

'I don't have it here,' I told Thing, as I went to close the window. 'It's on my mum's mobile, which is downstairs somewh— OW!'

I'd been splatted – and splatted *hard*!

'HA HA HA!' came a gurgle of laughter from the window right opposite mine.

I glowered over at Jackson's open bedroom window – no one was there.

But I *could* see a missing scoop of snow on the sill.

Actually, there were TWO missing scoops in the snow.

Uh-oh.

'FNAR!!' snorted Matt, appearing in view with . . .

1. a cackling Luke right beside him, and

2. his arm bent in aim.

'Don't you *dare* throw that sn—'

As soon as I called out, the next snowball came hurtling towards me.

I dodged to the left, and it whizzed past my ear and landed somewhere in the room.

'Hey, guys!' Jackson said with a smirk, as he joined his cousins. 'It's better not to go near her. Remember, she's a bit crazy!'

Jackson crossed his eyes and spun his finger beside his head.

'HA HA HA HA HA!!' cackled Luke.

'HUH HUH HUH HUH!' snorted Matt.

I guessed Jackson was just trying to carry on with the story he'd spun in the garden last night.

But being talked about and laughed at *hurts*.

Specially when you're suddenly not so sure your friend is acting in a friendly way. (I didn't like that smirk at *all*.)

'Anyway, c'mon, let's go to the park and

get sledging, yeah?' I heard Jackson say now.

It seemed I definitely WASN'T invited.

Not that I'd want to go with smirking
Jackson Miller and his stupid cousins anyway.

SLAM!!

I shut the window *so* hard it was a wonder
the glass didn't smash.

But I did hear *another* sound I didn't much
like . . .

'EEEEEEEEK!!'

There, in the middle of the rug, was the
snowball. And it had grown legs and arms.
Furry red legs and arms, which were flapping
wildly.

So THAT'S where it had landed!

I fell to my knees and scraped all the iciness off Thing.

'Snowblob – it try to *eat* me!' it coughed, moon eyes wider than wide in terror.

'No, it wasn't eating you, it was jus—'

'Snowblob very, *very* bad, Rubby!' Thing spluttered on, trembling with upset and rage. 'It very, very, very, very, *very* bad!'

Help . . .

Spling!

Yep, the seriously spectacular weirdness was starting.

Spling! Spling!

Sparkles twinkled and danced in front of my eyes . . .

Thing's rubbish magic was filling my room, and this time – with no Frodo there to lick Thing happy – there was nothing I could do to stop it.

Flickers of light danced round us, as if someone had set off a sparkler, and that sparkler had gone cartwheeling off, bouncing from wall to wall.

Then, just as soon as this amazing mini fireworks show started, it stopped.

'Thing?'

Before the magic, my fuzzy friend had lain trembling on my rug.

Now, *after* the magic, it clung to my chest like a freaked-out monkey baby, just staring, staring.

In fact we stared and stared together, around my dazzlingly bright room. On the windowsill, on the desk, on the dressing table, on *every single surface* were propped dozens and dozens of mobile phones, *all* with a Diwali candle glowing in their screens.

Knock, knock, knock . . .

'Ruby?' Mum's voice called from the other side of the door. 'Everything OK? I heard a crash!'

Now it was my turn to go 'EEEEEEEEEK!!'

What if Mum came in? How could I explain the fact that her mobile had duplicated itself over and *over* and over again?

'I'm fine!' I lied, holding Thing tight and feeling its heart thump at top speed, same as mine. 'A gust of wind blew my window closed!'

As soon as I said those words, I realised *that* could be the answer to our sudden, flickering problem.

'Oh, no worries!' Mum said, before the pad of her footsteps told me she was walking away.

'Quick!' I hissed to Thing. 'We need to blow, blow, blow!!'

'Blow! Yes, blow is *good*, Rubby!' Thing agreed.

And so together we ran round the room huffing and puffing, blowing out every flame – and every conjured-up mobile with it.

We huffed and puffed some more, till our lungs ached and there was nothing left on the surfaces except a few wisplets of smoke and a spark or two of disappearing magic.

In fact, if my room had been a birthday cake, I think I blew out enough fake flames to be aged two hundred and three ...

Angels and dingbats

Mum stared at me.

Dad stared at me.

Luckily enough, they were both staring at my face, and didn't seem to notice the Thing-sized lump in the hood of my hoodie.

'Are you *sure* you don't want one of us to take you to the park today?' asked Mum.

'I'm sure,' I told her.

'Are you *sure* you're not upset Jackson's going there with his cousins and not inviting you?'

'I'm sure,' I told him.

'Are you *sure* you just want to play on your own in the garden?' asked Mum.

'I'm sure,' I told them both.

Mum and Dad looked at each other. They thought I was telling little white lies. They were sure I was a bit wibbly cos of Jackson, his parents, his nan and cousins all trooping out of the house with the sledge this morning, leaving me behind.

'I HONESTLY don't mind!' I tried to assure them.

Thing and I, we'd had a lovely time in my room just now – once we'd got our breath back after the huffing and puffing.

We'd made more plastic snowflake

bunting (it looked quite realistic, in a crinkly sort of way).

I'd explained the point of socks (Thing found one on the floor and mistook it for a hat).

And we'd tickled Christine's paws so that she looked liked she was running in her sleep (*way* too funny).

But my furry friend's tummy said it was

lunch o'clock, so it was time to smuggle Thing safely back to the trees and its stash of mushrooms.

'Well, if you're *sure*, Ruby,' Mum said one last time, 'then that would work for me – I could do with nipping off to the shops for an hour.'

'And *I* could do with getting on with that report I've got to write,' Dad joined in.

'Don't worry about me! I'll be fine!' I called out, leaving them to it and opening the back door.

The world outside was dazzlingly, perfectly white.

The thick duvet of snow on the grass lay untouched by foot (or paw) prints.

Sunlight twinkled through the glassy icicles swaying from branches in the brittle, *brrrr* air.

And best of all, no one was around.

'Hey, Thing,' I said a few minutes later, when we were hunkered down in the trees.

'Yes, *please*, Rubby?' Thing asked, finishing off its mushroomy meal with a delicate burp.

'How about we play in my garden for a while!'

'It *safe*, Rubby?' said Thing, widening its bushbaby eyes in surprise.

'Well, Mum is out, and once Dad gets on the computer it's like he's been sucked into the Internet,' I joked.

Thing looked a bit worried, and I remembered it didn't really *get* jokes.

'Doesn't matter,' I said quickly, before Thing asked where the Internet was exactly and why it wanted to eat my dad. 'Anyway, everyone's out next door too. And if we stay hidden behind the shed, we'll be fine!'

Thing didn't need convincing after that.

I could tell, because it had scrambled over the wall before I'd even straightened myself up.

'Peh!'

But Thing *should've* waited for me, since it found itself chest-deep in a snowdrift on the other side.

'Come here,' I laughed. 'I've got an idea . . .'

And with that, I took off my fleecy hoodie

and put it on back to front.

After a few seconds of struggling to do my zip up at the back, I was ready with my lookalike baby sling

'Like it?' I asked, popping Thing into the hood, facing out.

'Hee, hee!' Thing giggled, as it watched me rack up a row of tiddly snow 'peoples' along the garden wall.

'That *my* name?' it gasped, as I wrote 'Thing' with my finger on the frosted shed window.

'Now I do *Rubby* name!' it announced, leaning forward and scratching out a random squiggle that looked *exactly* like a random squiggle.

'I do *weather*!' it declared, as we stood beside the huge rhododendron bush and shook the branches to make our own mini snowstorm.

'Ooh, I've just thought of something *else*!' I said, brimming with happiness.

Me and Thing, we were having such a good time on our own.

Who needed Jackson? Or his *smirk*?

'What is *else*, Rubby?' asked Thing, turning round in my cosy hood to face me.

'Snow angels!' I burst out.

Ever since I was as tiny as Thing (well, maybe not *quite* as tiny), I'd loved lying down, flapping about and ending up with an outline of me as an angel, complete with snowy wings.

'What is you *say*inging, Rubby?' Thing asked, not quite catching my words.

'Watch me!' I ordered it.

Without spilling Thing, I eased myself down on the ground, did a flip-flap, and stood up again.

'See?' I said, pointing.

'Yes, *please*! Rubby is *birdie*!' Thing purred. 'Now *I* be birdie?'

'Sure!' I said, without correcting it. (Trying to describe an angel would probably tie Thing's brain in knots.)

I stepped over to a new, untrampled-on patch of snow, then placed Thing down.

'Copy what I do,' I told it.

'I swimmin' in snow, Rubby!' Thing squeaked in pleasure, wafting its arms and legs at the same time. 'Wheee!'

'Wheee! WHEEEEEEEE!' I joined in.

'My! What a lot of fun's going on over here!' came an all-of-a-sudden voice.

I froze on the freezy ground.

A smiley face peered over the fence that separated Jackson's house from mine.

Jackson's nan!

What was she *doing* here?! I saw her leaving for the park with the others ages ago ...

Why was she holding something that looked like an old-fashioned tea cosy?

And most importantly, WHAT WAS SHE GOING TO DO NOW SHE'D SEEN THING!

Y'know, I always thought it would be *Jackson* who'd goof and spill the beans about Thing. But it turned out that *I* was the one who couldn't keep it safe from—

'Oh!' said Jackson's nan, looking at me, and looking surprised. 'I thought I heard more than one voice a second ago, but it's just *you*, dear ...'

What?

I tilted my head and saw only a Thing-shaped snow angel, which disappeared as I quickly swooshed it away with my hand.

'Um, nope, just me . . . goofing around!' I told Jackson's nan, as I pushed myself up to a sitting position.

'Right . . .' she answered dubiously, rubbing her glasses with the edge of her scarf. (She could rub all she liked, my fantastic little friend had scuttled into hiding before she'd caught a glimpse of it.)

'I, er, thought you went to the park with Jackson and his cousins?' I said, standing up, brushing myself down and trying to be polite.

'Well, Jackson forgot *this*, so I offered to pop back and get it,' his nan said with a smile, holding up the old-fashioned tea cosy. 'I knitted it specially for him.'

Gulp. So the tea cosy was a *hat*? No wonder Jackson had 'forgotten' it!

It was made of scratchy-looking beige wool, and had a skull and crossbones knitted into it in baby blue. The trouble was . . .

- 'beige' and 'baby blue' aren't very cool, pirate-y colours.
- Jackson's nan had stitched a wide, happy smile on to the skull, which didn't look very cool or pirate-y either.

'Then I decided not to rush, and have a cup of tea before I caught up with them,' she carried on. 'I was just standing at the back door, waiting for the kettle to boil, when I heard you giggling.'

Me; giggling and 'wheee!'ing on my own. Ha! Jackson's nan probably thought I was as much of a dingbat as his cousins already did.

233

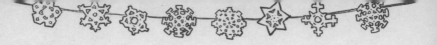

But to get her off the subject of what I
was doing, I decided to ask her a question.

'Why do Jackson's cousins call him
"Peanut"?'

'Ooh, he's had that nickname since they
were all little, but I can't think *how* it started!'
Jackson's nan said thoughtfully. 'Maybe
because Jackson loves peanut butter? Or
because he used to be as small as a peanut
compared with Matt and Luke?'

Well, I didn't think much of either of those
possible explanations. Mainly cos . . .

1. Jackson once told me he thought
   peanut butter was like eating salty
   wallpaper paste.

2. Since he was taller than Luke, the
   small-as-a-peanut suggestion just
   didn't work.

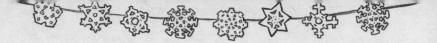

'I meant to say, Ruby,' Jackson's nan chattered on, 'your little ginger kitten is *adorable*!'

'My little ginger kitten?' I repeated, wondering what she was on about.

I didn't have a little ginger kitten.

I had a very, very old black and white cat.

'When we were leaving earlier, I popped up to Jackson's bedroom to get a jumper for Matt,' she carried on. 'I glanced over at your cottage and saw you through the window, playing in your room with your kitten. I think it was chasing some trailing white ribbon?'

That was no trailing white ribbon – that was plastic Christmassy bunting.

And that was no kitten – that was *Thing*!

'ExcusemeIhavetogoIthinkmydadneedsme,' I jabbered in a panic, suddenly desperate to get away.

'Oh! All right, dear!' I heard Jackson's nan's voice trail after me. 'But did you realise you had your top on back-to-front?'

'Ilikeitthatway!' I lied fast, and hurried off into my house.

Despite my heart thud-a-dudding, I realised I knew two important facts about Jackson's nan . . .

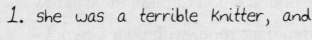

1. she was a terrible knitter, and

2. she **DEFINITELY** needed new glasses (luckily for Thing).

All of a sudden serious

BING-BONG! went the doorbell.

'I'll get it!' I shouted.

Well, Mum couldn't go, since she was in the bath.

And Dad was busy drying the Sunday breakfast dishes. (I'd already washed them.)

I didn't want to stop Dad doing his chores, since he'd promised that we'd go sledging together as soon as he was finished.

'Oh, hi!' I said, finding Jackson on my doorstep – with Frodo.

Forgetting for a second about Jackson's mean words (and meaner smirk), I felt pleased to see him. Frodo too.

I leaned forward and stroked his head.

Frodo's, I mean, not Jackson's.

Even if I'd *wanted* to stroke Jackson's head (ha!), I wouldn't have been able to, since he was wearing that AWFUL 'pirate' hat.

I couldn't help staring at it and grinning.

'Don't laugh,' he groaned, yanking it off and setting free his blond, spiky hair. 'My nan made it for me.'

'I know,' I giggled, as he stuffed the smiling skull in his jacket pocket. 'She told me yesterday.'

'Yeah, well, that's why I'm here,' said Jackson, all of a sudden serious.

'What's wrong?' I asked, feeling a bit anxious.

'How could you be so *dumb*, Ruby?' he
accused me. 'Nan said she saw you with a
"ginger kitten" in your room. She said it in
front of Mum and Dad, who *know* you don't
have a kitten. Guess what I had to do? I had
to tell them later that I thought Nan was
getting a little loopy, and that she must've
imagined it. That made me feel *really* bad.
But I had to cover up for you, since you

were stupid enough to play with Thing in your room where *anyone* could spot you!'

Wow.

That was a LOOOOONNNNGGGGG rant.

A LOOOOONNNNGGGGG rant that was completely unfair.

I mean, yesterday morning I'd heard Jackson say, 'C'mon let's go to the park!' to his cousins. So how was I to know it would take them ages to actually leave? And that his nan would come upstairs ten minutes later, noodling around for cosy jumpers?

Anyway, out of the two of us, *who* was more guilty of nearly letting Thing be discovered? *Loads* of times? Jackson 'It'll be all right!' Miller, *that's* wh—

'OI! PEANUT!! MOVE IT!' I heard a horrible cousin yell, and Jackson tugged at Frodo and sloped off without a backward glance.

Jackson, I mean. Frodo was staring back at me, wondering why I wasn't coming to play.

Grrr.

That was me growling, not Frodo.

So Jackson thought I couldn't look after Thing, did he?

Well, we'd see about *that*!

I slammed the door shut and stomped off indoors, fizzing with fury.

Actually, can I tell you something?

Making a plan when you are fizzing with fury is NOT a great idea.

As I was about to find out, in about, ooh, twenty minutes' time ...

9

Twenty minutes later . . .

'Where's your husky, Ruby?' asked Dad.

I narrowed my eyes at him as we walked through the park gates.

He was teasing me for sure, but I didn't know why.

'We're only going for a sledge in Victoria Park, you know,' said Dad with a grin. 'Not a three-month trek to the Arctic!'

OK, so he was joking about what I was wearing.

I don't mean my wellies or cosy coat or woolly hat and gloves; it was my scarf, wasn't it?

It *was* a bit big.

It was Mum's, actually.

It was one of those large, thin cotton scarves grown-up ladies like to wear, looped round and round their necks. The sort that are *so* humungous that they'd practically be the size of *bed sheets* if you unscrunched them and smoothed them all the way out.

Here's the thing about Mum's scarf; once I'd wound it round myself a few times, it made a perfect little hammock of material at my chest.

And guess who was cuddled up in that hammock?

Guess who was peering out through the

fine, patterned cotton, getting quite a good
– if blurry – view of the outside world, while
no one could see *it*?

'It's very fashionable!' I told Dad, then
giggled.

Now it was Dad's turn to frown at *me*.

He was wondering what the snigger was
for, but I could hardly tell him that Thing

had just squiggled about trying to get comfy. (All that squiggling with little claws was pretty tickly.)

'I'm just excited,' I fibbed, as we padded through the snow.

In front of us was a trail of people, either coming or going to the slope in the middle of the park.

You couldn't see the slope from here; it was just beyond the café and the ridge of trees.

But listen; the excited roars and *waaah*!s and *wheee*!s of sledgers drifted towards us.

I couldn't *wait* to join them!

Me and Dad would find a spot as far away from Jackson and his cousins as possible, and we'd hurtle downhill till we were all hurtled out.

Thing was going to have the best (secret) time *ever*, and tomorrow morning at school, I would shock Jackson by telling him that

Thing had been with me the whole time at the park.

He would be amazed, and probably slightly jealous of us having fun without him.

Which would serve him right since he hadn't been very nice to me since his horrible cousins had arrived . . .

'Yoo-hoo!' came a sudden call.

We turned and saw that it was Jackson's nan doing the yoo-hooing. She and Mr and Mrs Miller were sitting at an outdoor table by the café, hugging hot chocolates.

'Hello!' said Dad, steering me and the sledge over in their direction.

Within about a nanosecond, the adults were all chit-chattering away together, in the way adults do. The way that is really, REALLY irritating for their children, who have to hover politely and not moan, not even a little bit.

Jackson's nan seemed to spot my 'oh-no-they're-going-on-and-on-and-*on*' bored shuffle.

'Why don't you go and get sledging, Ruby?' she suggested. 'Jackson and the boys are already there.'

'Yeah, Ruby?' said Dad. 'You want to do that, and I'll catch you up in a couple of minutes?'

'OK,' I replied, glad to get away, even though I had no intention of looking for 'Peanut' and his mates.

Dragging my red sledge along the path of to-ing and fro-ing footprints, I put one hand to my chest so Thing wouldn't jiggle about too much.

'Here we are!' I mumbled to the bump in my scarf, as we cleared the ridge of trees and found ourselves at the top of the swoosh-tastic slope.

Beside us were rows of kids and parents,

lining up to take their turn zooming and shrieking.

I scanned the place, on the lookout for Jackson, but it was too crowded to make him or his cousins out. (Good.)

'Ready?' I whispered, as I got myself settled in the sledge, about to push off.

'I *ready*, Rubby!' Thing purred softly back.

'Here we gooooOOOOOOOO!!!!' I yelped as we whizzed off at top speed.

'Wheeeeeeeeee!' came a weedy, high-pitched yelp from my scarf.

'WHEEEEEEEE!' I yelped louder, just to cover it up.

'BARK! BARK! BARK! BARK! BARK!' woofed a blur of black and white, suddenly running alongside us.

It was Frodo!

Which meant Jackson *had* to be somewhere close by.

As we slithered to a stop at the bottom of
the slope, the dopey dog leaped on to the
sledge and practically burrowed his nose in
my scarf.

Yikes – it could smell Thing!

'Calm down!' I told Frodo, as I scrabbled
to my feet and pushed him off my chest.

'BARK! BARK!' barked Frodo, jumping
right back up again.

But suddenly he flopped to his feet, tilting

his furry head and cocking a fluffy ear.

He was listening to a panting sound.

A panting sound that was coming from the hammock on my chest.

'What did you just say to Frodo?' I mumbled to the scarf, checking noone was within hearing distance.

'I say "Be nice, *not* jump, *not* scare girl",' purred Thing.

'But I'm not scared for myself, Thing,' I mumbled. 'I'm scared for *you*, in case Frodo yanked the scarf and you tumbled out. We can't risk you getting discovered!'

'Yes, *please*, Rubby,' Thing replied from deep inside the bundle of material. 'But Dog not understandinging all that *blah, blah, blah*. Dog my friend, but *tiny* bit stupid.'

Fair enough.

I felt the same way about Jackson.

And spook!

Here was a coincidence; I was just thinking about my so-called friend, when a big baboon in a baby blue, smiley pirate hat lurched up in front of me.

'Ruby!' Jackson said with a friendly grin. 'You're here!'

Wait a minute.

When I saw him earlier, he was horribly cross with me.

Yesterday, he was saying really mean things about me to his cousins.

On Friday he sounded completely bored when he was introducing me to them.

It was hard enough to be friends with the normal, nice-but-dim version of Jackson.

All these different versions of him were making me very confused. *More* confused than the time I tried to explain how voices came out of mobiles to Thing. ('Very *little* peoples stuck in phonie, Rubby?')

'Look,' said Jackson, shuffling and sounding embarrassed. 'I'm sorry if—'

I didn't get to hear the rest of his apology. It was drowned out by a shout.

'Whooo–OOOO–oooo! PEANUT'S TALKING TO HIS *GIRLFRIEND*!'

Jackson's head dropped to his chest.

'I keep *telling* them you're not my girlfriend!' he said wearily.

I glanced over his shoulder at Luke and Matt, who were over by the closed-for-winter ice-cream booth, grinning in a non-friendly way.

'PEANUT'S IN LOVE! AW!!' yelled Matt.

'Why do they call you that name?' I asked Jackson, anger burbling in my chest. (And a scrabbling too – Thing could feel my heart pounding, for sure.)

'When I was about five, they held me

down and stuck a peanut up my nose,' said Jackson, his head still hanging. 'It was jammed up there till my auntie made me sniff enough pepper to sneeze it out . . .'

All of a sudden, I realised something.

Something that explained Jackson's not-so-nice behaviour.

My friend had been acting all kinds of strange with me because he was ever so slightly *scared* of his bossy, horrid cousins.

They were nothing but bullies!

Without knowing what I was about to say or do I started marching towards Luke and Matt, with Frodo barking at my side.

'LOOK OUT! WEIRD GIRL COMING OUR WAY!!' cackled Luke.

'RETREAT!' shouted Matt, disappearing around the side of the ice-cream booth.

'What *happening*, Rubby?' purred Thing. 'Your chest go BUH-doom, BUH-doom!'

'I've just got to tell some stupid boys to keep their stupid mouths shut!' I muttered darkly, as I stomped closer to the wooden building.

'Ruby? Ruby, don't!' came Jackson's voice, trailing somewhere behind me.

But a big red storm of **AARGHH!** was whirling in my head and my ears, and I didn't pay any attention to my friend's warning.

Instead, I found myself on the far side of the ice-cream booth and saw Luke and Matt standing in front of a giant *mega*-snowman that must've been at least two metres high.

'EEEEK!' came a high-pitched squeak from my chest.

'SCARED?' laughed Matt, assuming *I'd* made that noise, and not the Thing hiding in my scarf hammock. 'WELL, YOU *SHOULD* BE! HA HA HA!!'

Thud!

Thwack!

Doof!

I was hit by a splatter of snowballs, *all* of them hard – and they kept coming. The boys must've made a mountain of them.

'Ouch!' squeaked my chest, as it took a direct hit.

Help! The icy missiles were coming so fast and furious that all I could do was fall on my knees and curl up in a ball to protect myself and Thing.

'Not *like* giant *snow peoples*, Rubby! It scary!' Thing squeaked in a panic, as we huddled nose to nose. 'And not *like* snowblobs! They *very* cold and hurty!'

'It'll be OK,' I whispered reassuringly, as thumps *thudd*ed, *thwack*ed and *doof*ed on my back.

But it wasn't about to be OK any time soon, even though I could hear Jackson calling for his cousins to stop, over the top of Frodo's frantic barking.

The reason I was so sure was because my chest had begun to vibrate.

Thing was trembling.

Uh-oh . . .

A sparkle lit up the cramped hollow of my chest and arms.

Spling!

Yep, the seriously spectacular weirdness was starting.

'Thing!' I whispered. 'Please don't!'

Spling! Spling!

It was too late. Sparkles twinkled and danced in front of my face, so bright I had to squeeze my eyes tight shut.

cRACKLE
sPiT
FIZZZZzzZ!!

The sound of Thing's rubbish magic was filling my ears and there was nothing I could do to stop it.

'WHAT – WHAT'S *HAPPENING*?' I vaguely heard a panicked shout from one of Jackson's cousins.

I bet flickers of light were spilling all round me, as if I'd set off a sparkler, and that sparkler had gone cartwheeling off, bouncing around on the snowy ground and into the freezing air.

Then, just as soon as this amazing mini fireworks show started, it stopped.

Slowly, I unfurled myself, and found Jackson beside me, helping me up.

'You brought *Thing* here?' he whispered.

'Mmm. Who saw?' I muttered back.

'Cos of the ice-cream booth, the magic was hidden from everyone up on the slopes,'

Jackson pointed out. 'No one saw it except *those* two . . .'

Those two were Luke and Matt, of course.

Both boys stood gawping at their giant mega-snowman, which was looking a *lot* different all of a sudden.

'HOW . . . ?' Matt gasped, his eyes fixed on a neat mound of snowballs where the snowman had stood seconds before.

'Well done, Thing!' I muttered into my chest, patting at the fabric.

But, EEEK!

There was nothing there to pat!!

The scarf . . . it was *empty*.

I gazed up at Jackson, who understood straight away.

He twisted and turned, looking this way and that.

'Frodo!' he said suddenly, pointing off towards a black and white and blur, which

was disappearing into the trees, a lead trailing behind it.

The blur – it wasn't *totally* black and white. There was a splodge of *ginger* in there too!

Together, we began to run.

Except those shrieks; they made us both hesitate and glance behind us.

'OW! OW! *AH!!*'

'NO! HELP! *OUCH!!*'

*Un*making the snowman wasn't the *whole* of Thing's magic.

The neat mound of snowballs; they'd risen up and were now whirling in the air, *then went thundering down on* Jackson's cousins.

'AH! OW! OOF!' they both yelped.

Jackson turned to me.

We just had time for a quick smile and a high-five before we hurried after our runaway dog and Thing . . .

Getting hot and being cool

'Looking for this fella?' Dad called out, as me and Jackson sprinted breathlessly towards the café and the exit to the park.

Dad was standing right where I'd left him, beside the table where Jackson's mum, dad and nan were still hugging their mostly finished hot chocolates.

By his feet was a panting Frodo, in his hand Frodo's lead.

'I think he, er, got spooked by something and took off!' Jackson explained quickly.

Meanwhile, I dropped to my knees, whispering, 'Good dog!' to Frodo, but wishing he could tell me more about his brave rescue operation. Like where exactly Thing *was* right now.

'Frodo popped up from under the table!' Jackson's mum said chattily.

'Probably sniffing about for food!' Jackson's dad chipped in, pointing to crumbs of muffin on a plate in front of him.

The table . . .

I dipped my head down a little – and saw a flash of red fur!

There was Thing, clinging to a supporting metal bar underneath the tabletop. It looked exactly like a small, worried sloth.

If its huge moon eyes could talk, they'd be saying 'Help! Help! Help!' for sure.

'I'm a bit hot now after all that running,' I muttered to no one in particular, unwrapping my scarf and casually chucking it down on the ground.

But no one in particular was listening to me anyway; they were all calling out to Luke and Matt, laughing at just how snow-splattered they were.

'Yoo hoo!' trilled their nan. 'You two look like you've been having a good time!'

Unseen by anyone but me and a sniffy Frodo, Thing scuttled down from its perch and disappeared under the folds of the fabric.

'What's up, boys? You look like you've seen a ghost!' laughed Mrs Miller as her two nephews ran ashen-faced – as well as snow-splattered – towards us.

I quickly gathered up the scarf (and its occupant) and cuddled it in my arms.

'WE GOT HIT BY ALL THESE SNOWBALLS!' babbled Luke.

'Sounds like fun!' said Mr Miller.

'IT WASN'T – *NO ONE* WAS THROWING THEM!' Matt added.

'Yeah, *right*,' my dad joined in with their 'joke'.

'NO, HONEST! OUR SNOWMAN TURNED INTO A PILE OF SNOWBALLS!' said Luke. 'AND THERE WAS A SORT OF TORNADO AND THEY *FLEW* AT US!'

'Wow, *really*?' Mr Miller laughed. 'I'd love to have seen that!'

'IT WAS *HER* FAULT!' Matt announced, pointing at me. 'IT ALL HAPPENED WHEN *SHE* TURNED UP! IT'S LIKE SHE'S A *WITCH* OR SOMETHING!'

'Now, boys, you're getting a little bit silly,'
said their nan, her indulgent smile slipping
a bit.

'IT'S TRUE!'

'YEAH, *TELL* 'EM, PEANUT!'

Jackson looked from one cousin to the
other. And for the first time, it looked like
they were nervous and *he* was in control.

'It was just a dumb game we were all playing,' Jackson said with a casual shrug and a wide baboon grin.

Yay — that was my Jackson! *My* friend! My friend who wasn't getting bossed about by his irritating, bully-boy cousins!

Luke and Matt; they were opening and shutting their mouths, not sure what to say or do.

If they kept insisting that their snowman had turned itself into flying snowblobs, or that I was a weirdo witch (ha!) they'd sound completely mad.

And worse, they'd *look uncool*.

So the brothers did the only thing they could — they stared warily at Jackson and grudgingly agreed with him.

'Uh, yeah,' grunted Matt, not shouting for once. 'It's like Peanut said . . .'

'Hey, and I don't like being called Peanut,'

Jackson added, getting confident now and twirling his knitted hat round his finger. 'Can you stop doing that?'

'Yeah, whatever,' Matt muttered, as Luke nervously nodded beside him.

'Oh, I *love* that you all get along so well!' said Nan, getting up from her chair and giving them all an embarrassing, squelchy granny kiss one by one.

That sure wiped the confident grin off Jackson's face.

Though not as much as when his nan grabbed the twirling hat from his finger and shoved it on to his blond hair.

'There. Don't want my darling grandson to catch a chill now, do we?'

It was only then that I realised *all* the boys had matching hats.

As the three baby blue skulls smiled down at me, I giggled and giggled and giggled till everyone thought I was a complete dingbat.

But since most of them thought I was a
dingbat already, who cared . . . ?

The never-
mind-cuddle

Frodo lay flopped over the tree roots, tired after an exciting day being walked, lost and found.

It was Sunday afternoon, and me and Jackson had just waved off his tearful nan and his sheepish cousins.

'See you next time, Jacko!' Matt had called out, while Luke looked fairly scared still, and Jackson had beamed at his new, improved nickname.

'Another jelly baby, Ruby?' he asked now, lounging on the black plastic bin liner I'd laid over the snow like a waterproof picnic blanket.

'Yes, thanks,' I said brightly, pausing as I stretched the carrier-bag snowflake bunting above him.

Soon, me and Jackson would have to take our part-time, woofy pet back to its real owners. But in the meantime, we were chilling out, having a sweetie snack and watching Thing attempt to make its new nest.

Since Thing was busy, I took a couple of jelly babies from the packet Jackson was holding out and popped them into its new special dishy.

(Tomorrow I'd tell Miss Wilson that I'd dropped and broken the diva. Though it was looking very pretty now, covered in glittery stickers that came free with my latest copy of *Girls Are Us!* magazine.)

'Peh!' came a sigh from inside the Mystery
Machine.

'Is the bedding no good, d'you think?'
Jackson asked me, nodding down at his old
toy, buried under bracken.

'Not sure,' I replied.

The late-afternoon sun was glowing
and golden out in the garden. But here,
under the trees, the light was fading fast

. . . time to switch on the pumpkin. (I'd finally found my Halloween torch on my bedroom floor under my chucked-down copy of *Girls Are Us!*.)

'Peh!' muttered Thing, its fuzzy red back visible at the open doors of the van as it pushed and squeezed and *squizzled* its bedding into place.

'Don't you like it, Thing?' asked Jackson, as me, him and Frodo all peered at what was going on.

What a shame. So far, Thing had tried . . .

- moss (too soft).

- leaves (too scratchy).

- sponge (too sproingy).

- empty jelly-baby packets (too rustly).

. . . and now Jackson's *latest* offering, which by the sound of it, wasn't cosy and crunchy enough either.

'Peh!' purred Thing, shuffling round to face us.

It wrung its little paws together, tiny tears streaming down its furry face.

Frodo whined, and wriggled towards his small sad friend.

'Hey, don't be upset, Thing!' said Jackson, sounding pretty upset himself.

'We can try out some more stuff!' I added, reaching over to scoop up Thing and give it a never-mind-cuddle.

'But I not *sad*, Rubby!' it sniffed, blinking up at me. 'I happy! Jackson's mess *best* mess I ever have!'

It was then that I realised 'peh!' can mean a fed up sort-of-sigh, OR a hurray-for-my-new-cosy-crunchy-*nest* sort-of-sigh.

It was also when Jackson realised that there was a very good use for his awful, nan-knitted, smiling skull-and-crossbones hat after all.

'Can we do big *huggly*?' asked Thing, holding out its arms.

Now that life was back to our weird kind of normal, having a huggly with my three best friends (one a doggy, one a donut and one a special secret) was exactly what I wanted to do.

'C'mere!' I said, squeezing all three so tight that Thing giggled and squealed, Frodo wriggled and barked, and Jackson accidentally kissed me on the cheek . . .*

(Yuck.†)

---

* It definitely WAS by accident, right?
† I, er, KIND of kissed him back. By accident too. (Double yuck!)